"This book devastated me in the most wonderful way. Beck and Sela are so scorching and real together that I didn't want to let them go. I can't wait to devour the rest of this series!"
—#1 *New York Times* bestselling author MEREDITH WILD

"A totally gripping take on romance and revenge!"
—*New York Times* bestselling author LAUREN BLAKELY

"*Sugar Daddy* is raw, gritty, and exceptionally hot. I couldn't put it down."
—*New York Times* bestselling author MARQUITA VALENTINE

"Wow! Sawyer Bennett steps out of her ice skates and into her Manolos. *Sugar Daddy* is a hot read that only gets better with every page." —*New York Times* bestselling author SUSAN STOKER

"I read it in less than three hours because I am a freak reader when I like something. This book is great!"
—*USA Today* bestselling author MJ FIELDS

"Sawyer Bennett has talent that knows no bounds and this book proves it. From page one to the end I was captivated and enthralled. I can't wait for more!"
—*USA Today* bestselling author CHELSEA CAMARON

"Sawyer Bennett does dark with amazing facility, drawing me in with Sela's story, and holding me there with Beck's. *Sugar Daddy* is compulsively readable, deliciously dirty, and passionately written." —*USA Today* bestselling author CD REISS

"Sawyer Bennett delivers a titillating novel that balances between the desire to seek revenge and the yearning to hold on to love. It's sexy and addicting, and I devoured every last word."
—MEGHAN QUINN, author of *The Randy Romance Novelist*

By Sawyer Bennett

COLD FURY HOCKEY SERIES

Alex
Garrett
Zack
Ryker
Hawke
Max (coming soon)

SUGAR BOWL

Sugar Daddy
Sugar Rush
Sugar Free

THE WICKED HORSE SERIES

Wicked Fall
Wicked Lust
Wicked Need
Wicked Ride
Wicked Bond

THE OFF SERIES

Off Sides
Off Limits
Off the Record

Off Course
Off Chance
Off Season
Off Duty

THE LAST CALL SERIES

On the Rocks
Make It a Double
Sugar on the Edge
With a Twist
Shaken, Not Stirred

THE LEGAL AFFAIRS SERIES

Legal Affairs
Confessions of a Litigation God
Friction
Clash
Grind
Yield

STANDALONE TITLES

If I Return
Uncivilized
Love: Uncivilized

Sugar
Rush

Sugar Rush

A SUGAR BOWL NOVEL

SAWYER
BENNETT

LS

LOVESWEPT
NEW YORK

A Loveswept Trade Paperback Original

Published in the United States by Loveswept, an imprint of Random House, a division of Penguin Random House LLC, New York.

LOVESWEPT is a registered trademark and the LOVESWEPT colophon is a trademark of Penguin Random House LLC.

This book contains an excerpt from the forthcoming book *Max* by Sawyer Bennett. This excerpt has been set for this edition only and may not reflect the final content of the forthcoming edition.

ISBN 978-0-399-17859-7
Ebook ISBN 978-1-101-96813-0

Printed in the United States of America on acid-free paper

randomhousebooks.com

1 2 3 4 5 6 7 8 9

Book design by Elizabeth A. D. Eno

Thank you Sue, Gina, and Matt for taking a chance on me and continuing to make me a better author with each book we put out.

Sugar
Rush

. . . .

CHAPTER 1

Sela

*I throw all caution to the wind and I bare my soul to him. "JT . . .
he raped me."*

Cold eyes.

Look of disgust.

"Yet another lie, Sela."

Then he slams the door in my face.

Pain such as I've never felt seizes my chest.

It's like a blackened claw wrapping around my heart, squeezing so hard it robs me of my breath. Squeezing and pushing out every bit of goodness and hope and light. I try to suck in oxygen but my lungs don't move. The cramping sensation in my chest gets tighter, until I think I actually may be having a heart attack.

I'm on my hands and knees, with one arm reaching out toward our door.

Correction.

Beck's door.

Not mine anymore.

I wait, and then wait some more for him to open it back up, my chest caving in on itself.

And I wait.

My head drops, hair falling in a curtain as I stare at the dark gray carpeting. My arm succumbs to gravity and my palm presses down for balance. I remember to that moment when I first saw JT on TV and vomited all over my threadbare carpet. Back then, I had been assaulted with terrifying memories that I realized were not just nightmares but waking, living, breathing events that had happened me. I was caught under an avalanche of fear and shame and self-loathing. I vomited and cried and expelled snot all over the carpet.

Not this time.

Right now, my eyes are bone-dry and I know this is because my body is shutting down, refusing to accept the magnitude of what I just lost. If I really consider everything that Beck is to me, and that I will no longer have it again, I'm not sure I'll physically survive it.

I'm sure that if I give credence to the fact that I just destroyed every bit of trust and care he had for me, my heart will end up curling in on itself. It will form into a dried-out, blackened knot of bitterness that I'll never overcome, and it will be far worse than any pain I've experienced in my life.

Yes, even more painful than *that*, and I don't have it in me for that type of suffering again.

So I have to push past . . . ignore . . . obliviate.

Lurching up onto my knees, I place my hands on my thighs for balance, and try once again to catch a breath. Grudgingly, my lungs expand and pull precious life into me and I let it out in a quavering sigh of defeat.

My gaze falls to the floor again, and I see that the contents of my purse have been scattered clear across the hall. I take in another deep breath, feel my heart still cramping in agony.

God, it hurts.

So much.

My heart, my chest, my head.

My lungs.

My bones. I even feel the crushing weight of defeat and loss in my bones.

Reaching out, I grab the strap of my purse and pull it in to me. I look into the gaping opening and see my wallet and key chain still inside. I pull the keys out and work off Beck's condo key. It takes me a moment and I realize I'm clumsily fumbling with it because I feel dizzy.

I consciously pull in another lungful of oxygen, realizing that the pain just on the other side of my breastbone is so all consuming it's taken away my body's natural ability to want to live. To even pull in the basic necessity of the air I need to survive.

Deep breath in.

Let it out.

In.

Out.

Breathe, Sela. Just fucking breathe.

An agonized sob pops out of my mouth as images of Beck's face flash before me. His look so angry and condemning. His unwillingness to give me five precious minutes to explain myself. I jerk the key from the ring and fling it at the door, a sudden burst of anger filling me up and giving me strength.

Just as fast it gushes out of me.

And for a brief, glorious moment, my chest relaxes . . . the cramping fades. I take in a tentative breath and find my lungs expand easily. A swirling sensation of relief, and I use the opportunity to stand.

I keep still, afraid some other nasty or wretched emotion will take me hostage. I wait for it to come, to make my knees buckle, but . . . nothing.

I feel absolutely nothing.

"Beck," I *begged with a sob. "JT . . . he raped me."*

He hesitated, eyes wide with shock and face draining of blood. I even reached out to him, not once doubting that he'd want to help me.

But then my world crashed again when he looked down upon me with disgust and said, "Yet another lie, Sela," before slamming the door on me.

I think about Beck just moments ago, pushing me out his door, looking at me with disgust and calling me—the rape victim—a liar.

And nothing.

Absolute emptiness within me, but it's actually a blissful feeling, because it doesn't hurt.

My gaze falls back down to the carpet. Lip gloss, loose change, tampons, chewing gum, and a matchbook I took from a jazz club that Beck and I went to. A keepsake, so to speak.

Tiny cramp in my chest. I push it away and face the elevator, ignoring all of the scattered items.

I turn my back and leave it all behind.

All of it.

Behind.

CHAPTER 2

. . . .

Beck

The minute the door slams shut, blocking Sela and her treacher-
ous, lying eyes, I fall back against it. I immediately slump down to
the floor, my legs splayed out in front of me, toes tilted outward,
and my hands sit like useless lumps on my thighs.

When I first saw Sela sitting in my office, I was filled with rage
such as I've never known. It was blistering hot and my ears were
buzzing with static as adrenaline pumped like acid in my veins.

I knew.

Immediately knew she had lied to me about needing to take a
walk that day after Thanksgiving because she was overwhelmed. I
quickly figured out that she had taken my key chain and had a
copy made so she could get into my office. It tied together nicely.

How could I have been so stupid? How could I not have seen
the duplicity?

How in the fuck did I get played so well?

My body went on autopilot, my brain refusing to accept a
single word she said, because she's a proven liar, and I hate liars
more than anything. Hate fucking secrets and gray areas and deception and cover-ups. My parents taught me well to hate it, cre-

ating such a vile environment for what masqueraded as a family that they unwittingly made a man with no tolerance.

I'm sure lies continued to drip from her mouth even after I caught her. Hell, I'm not even sure what she was saying as I pulled her through the condo; my only concern was getting her out of my life. Rage, fury, bitterness . . . it was all the fuel I needed to push her right out, as I realized that Sela was not only playing with my life, she was playing with my heart.

As I sit here, feeling as if I don't have a single ounce of strength within me, I realize that as the mania subsides, I'm left with a desolate emptiness. Just minutes ago, I was full of Sela, and now there's a hollowness surrounded by a bitter husk.

I hear a sound on the other side of the door, and of course I know it's Sela.

A hoarse bark of a sound . . . a pained sob perhaps? An attempt to get me to feel bad about what I've done?

My fingers curl inward, press into my palms, and I have to push hard against the overwhelming need to open that door to comfort her.

I push up off the floor and stalk through the living room, trying to get as far away from the door and the sound of Sela crying. I cross my arms over my stomach, hugging myself almost protectively, and pace back and forth along the floor-to-ceiling window that overlooks the bay.

Something hits the door. A tinny sound, barely noticeable, and my head jerks that way. I take a step in that direction and halt myself.

Turn back around, face the window.

My body tenses, waiting to hear something else. Maybe Sela isn't done and will start trying to call out to me through the door. Maybe she'll try to throw more fiction at me, and in fact, maybe that's why she's silent right now. Her brain is working up a new web of deceit in which she'll try to capture me.

I wait and I wait, yet I don't hear anything else.

Please, Sela . . . say something and make a liar out of my feelings right now.

Dropping my arms, I walk hesitantly to the door and lean so my ear is placed against it. I don't hear a sound. I put my eye to the peephole, bracing myself to see Sela curled into some pitiful fetal position.

There's no one in the hallway, although I can't see all the way down to the elevator. For all I know, Sela's waiting there, ready to spring out at me.

I think about her last words. Those I do remember.

"JT raped me."

My teeth gnash over the ludicrousness of that statement. While I haven't spent every waking minute with Sela, I've spent enough time with her to know that couldn't have occurred. Not only was there very little opportunity, but I think I'd fucking well know if something horrific like that had happened to my girl-friend.

I know what rape does to a woman. I've seen it.

Fuck, I've felt it. I've felt a woman sobbing and shuddering in my arms, sunk in despair and pain after she was brutalized. JT is a shit, an abuser of women, and I'm not sure to what lengths he'd go anymore. But there's no fucking way JT raped Sela in the past several weeks we've been together. I would have absolutely known something was wrong. You can't hide something like that.

You can't.

I know the only fix is time, and that's not even a complete fix. A rape victim needs time and support and assurance. She needs love and the ability to work through the shame and humiliation. That shit doesn't happen in days. It doesn't happen in months.

It fucking happens in years.

And all of a sudden, something strikes out at me with such force and detailed clarity that I actually stagger back from the door a bit.

It's a memory of Sela on the first night we met.

Sitting on a barstool and staring across the room at JT.

With anger.

I remember seeing it clearly on her face, and thinking it was odd that she'd be staring at him that way. I had assumed that night was the first time Sela had met JT, and that's why it was so weird that she'd be looking at him that way.

Unless that wasn't the first time they met.

"JT raped me."

She didn't say when, did she?

My mind races as I try to recall the last ten minutes of my life and I can't pull forth anything. I can only remember her looking up at me, arm outstretched, as she said, *JT raped me.*

I assumed she meant since she and I had started up together. I assumed she was lying and inferring JT had done something nefarious, knowing my relationship with him has been strained and hoping I'd take her side over his. I immediately discounted her proclamation because I know what rape is, and there's no way in hell that could have happened since we met.

But what if he fucking raped her long before she and I ever met? What if she was at that Sugar Bowl Mixer that night with the intent to confront her attacker?

That first night we were together. Sela's juices on my mouth and her neck and chest flushed red from orgasm.

"That was the first time a man has made me have an orgasm."

Sela had not been able to orgasm with a man before.

It had seemed impossible to me then, knowing a beautiful, sexy, and vibrant woman like Sela couldn't attract a man who would bend over backward to make her come. No one could take one look at Sela lying on a bed, legs spread and eyes full of uncertainty but with a tinge of hope, and not do everything in his fucking power to make her come until she's screaming his name out to the heavens.

A woman not achieving climax with a man.

That's a serious sexual hang-up.

One that could be caused by being raped.

Everything hits me at once. I'm practically blinded by images and memories of the last few weeks, all little details that I can now piece together.

Sela's not your typical Sugar Baby. It's a ruse to get close to JT.

Sela's naïve when it comes to sex.

The aloof nature with which she held herself away from me.

The moments of uncertainty I saw on her face when we were intimate.

That absolute antipathy she had for JT the few times they've been in the same room together.

The fact I've come to see that JT has the potential to really harm a woman.

"I swear to God, Beck . . . this is about JT," she had cried out to me as I dragged her out of my condo.

Sela *was* raped by JT before we even met.

The absolute truth of that hits me square in the center of my chest with the force of a wrecking ball.

"F-u-u-u-u-ck," I groan painfully as I lunge for the door, absolutely sickened by what I've just done.

I jerk it open, my eyes immediately going to the array of items that I vaguely remember flying out of Sela's purse when I kicked it through the door. My head jerks to the right, toward the elevators, but she's gone. Her purse is gone, and she's gone, but she left behind all that shit that spilled out. My gaze drops down farther and I see the condo key with the blue rubber cover on the head of it.

It's like a kick to my nuts seeing it lying at my feet.

"No, no, no, no," I chant in agony as I squat to pick up the key. "Not you, Sela. This could not have happened to you. Not to *my* Sela."

I don't want to believe it because I literally don't think I can stand to know Sela suffered that way. I don't want to believe it because it makes me a monster for what I just did to her.

I stand up and pull my phone out of my pocket, quickly choosing Sela's number at the top of my favorites list. On the second ring, I note that I can faintly hear a corresponding sound coming from the bedroom.

"Shit," I mutter, and run back to our bedroom, where I see her phone lying on the nightstand beside the bed. I disconnect and look wildly about the room, trying to figure out what to do.

A quick glance down at my watch and I note that Sela couldn't have been gone for more than five minutes, ten at the most. She could still be down at the next BART stop, waiting for public transit to whisk her away from me.

I snatch Sela's phone from the nightstand and sprint for the front door. I pat my front pocket, relieved to feel my car key in there should I need it, and practically careen off the doorjamb as I try to cut into the hallway. I grab the knob and pull it shut hard behind me, not even stopping to lock up.

I have to catch Sela before she can get away.

Someone above is looking out for me because the elevator shows up within seconds. I jump in, jab the lobby button, and urge it to go faster. I start throwing up prayers to whoever may be listening to let me make this right with her. I'm so ashamed of the way I threw her out of my life, and how easily I discounted her claim of rape. It may be the worst mistake I've ever made, and I hope to God I can fix it.

When the elevator stops and the doors slide open with a soft *whoosh,* I bolt out and then turn left and dash for the front doors. I practically run over John, our doorman, and apologize to him as I hit the sidewalk.

The BART stop is one block down and half a block over, and luckily the sidewalks are fairly empty. It's past the morning rush hour but it hasn't hit lunchtime yet. I race around the corner of Mission and Fremont at a Mach 1 sprint, and my eyes immediately go to the bench in front of the bus stop. There's only two people there waiting, and neither of them are Sela.

My chest heaving for air, I look both ways down the street, desperately hoping to catch a glimpse of her. I squint, peer hard . . . willing her to appear.

Fuck . . . I can't even remember what she was wearing.

Totally fucking useless.

She's gone and I know it, so I start a slower paced jog back to my building. I utter another apology to John as I brush past him into the lobby, head over to the service stairwell, and take the stairs down one more flight to the garage. Sela has to be going to her apartment and I can easily beat her there by driving. I'll just be waiting at her front door for her, and hopefully by then I'll have something monumental figured out to undo this clusterfuck I've created.

CHAPTER 3

. . . .

Sela

TEN YEARS AGO . . .

"Bryce is such an asshole," Whitney says as she leans her elbows on the rail bordering the upper level of the mall. It overlooks the food court below, and the smell of greasy burgers and stale Chinese food filter upward. My nose crinkles in disgust.

"Agreed," I say as my eyes slowly roam around the upper level, checking out the action tonight. I'd already scanned the food court below, and nothing of interest was going on down there.

"He didn't say why?" she asks.

"Nope," I say calmly, although my stomach curdles when I think about the very public brush-off I got yesterday after school. Bryce and I had been dating for three months, and my face flushes with embarrassment when I think of all the proclamations of love I'd given him. He was my first real boyfriend in high school and I had fallen head over heels.

Bryce was very tall with sunny good looks that would have been common in Southern California, but only made him stand out like a beacon in our school in Menlo Park. He was the star of our basket-

ball team, every girl wanted to be with him, and every boy wanted to be him. Some of the best days of my life were spent just strutting through the hallways between periods, my hand grasped tightly in his as he'd walk me to my next class.

It was like a dream, and I was giddy, and happy, and in love.

And then he crushed me by dumping me after school in the parking lot standing outside the driver's door of his Mustang, surrounded by his buddies. I thought he'd be driving me home as he did every day after school since basketball season was over. Instead, he simply told me, "Listen, Sela . . . I want to break up."

I was stunned, and sure I heard him wrong. "What?"

"It's the end of my senior year. I'm heading off to college in a few months. I don't want to be tied down, especially not with a girl as young as you. You're not going to be able to hang with me and it will just be awkward, you know?"

No, I didn't know.

I didn't understand at all.

"But I'm sixteen," I told him lamely.

"Tomorrow you'll be sixteen," he pointed out, and one of his friends snickered loudly. At least Bryce had the grace to shoot him a dirty look and a small shake of his head.

"And you're breaking up with me the day before my birthday," I said in wonder and not to him in particular, and not a question either. Just a statement as to his douchiness.

Bryce just shrugged and reached for his car door. But then, as an afterthought, he said, "Look . . . you're a nice kid and everything . . ."

I tuned him out as I turned and walked away. That's all I needed to hear from him.

He thought I was a kid.

And now my eyes roam the busy Saturday night floors of the mall, bustling with shoppers and teens just hanging out, looking to have some fun. My eyes cut over to the Gap, directly across from me, and I see three guys walk out. All in jeans, T-shirts . . . look about my age, maybe a little older. Two of the guys are okay, but one is really cute. He's carrying a bag in his hand and laughs at something one of his friends says. He then pauses, takes his phone out of his back pocket, and answers it. His eyes travel left as he talks with a smile on his face, sweeps across the expanse of the mall, and then his gaze lands right on me.

While he converses with whoever is on the other line, he stares at me . . . lips quirked upward and eyes bright with interest. I smile back at him, conveying interest because he's really, really cute with light brown hair that's worn a bit long and what looks to be brown eyes.

My pulse starts fluttering when he ends the call, says something to his friends without taking his eyes off me, then starts heading my way across the bridge that connects to the opposite sides of the second story.

Whitney is rambling on about Bryce, something about wanting to crush his nuts in a vise, but I don't pay attention to her. He gets closer, his friends following a few steps behind him.

I can tell the minute that Whitney sees him because her voice trails off with a soft, "Oh, wow."

"Hey," he says when he stops a few feet from me. His eyes cut to Whitney and then back to me. While he doesn't overtly check me out, I can tell he likes what he sees. I'm thankful for my most flattering jeans and my mom's red heels I stole out of her bedroom before I left, hiding them in my large purse while walking out the door in sedate black flats. Those now reside in my bag and the red heels add four inches to my height.

"Hey," I say back, my eyes cutting down to his bag. "Good shopping?"

He shrugs, and it's very cool, I think. "Just killing time. We're getting ready to head out to a party."

"Cool," I say, hoping I sound cool and not lame.

"I'm Dallas," he says, and then nods to his friends. "That's David and Blake."

I turn slightly and grab Whitney's hand, pulling her forward to stand beside me. "This is Whitney . . . my best friend."

Dallas nods to her and his buddies turn away from us, both checking out their phones. Neither one of them looked at Whitney twice, which I don't get. She's really pretty with auburn hair and soft brown eyes.

But then Dallas makes me forget that when he leans in toward me and says, "Want to go to the party with us?"

"Where is it?" I ask casually, trying not to sound excited.

But I'm so excited. This is exactly what I was looking for tonight. Some type of validation that I'm interesting and worthy of a man's notice.

"It's over in Atherton," he says. "Some rich dude's house. My sister goes to college with him."

The way he says "rich dude" leads me to believe that Dallas is not rich himself, but that doesn't bother me. He's very cute and he looks at me like he doesn't see a kid.

"Sounds fun," I chirp at him. "Right, Whitney?"

"Um, I can't," Whitney says. "My curfew's at ten P.M."

Bummer. My parents said I could stay out until midnight since it was my birthday.

"Excuse me a minute," I say to Dallas, and pull Whitney five paces away. I lean in toward her and whisper, "Come on, Whitney. I really want to go. Call your mom and tell her you're staying the night with me."

She shakes her head and looks at me with worried eyes. "No way. Last time we tried that and got busted, I was grounded for a week. And besides . . . we don't know these guys."

My eyes cut over to Dallas, who is looking down at his phone.

So freakin' cute. Way cuter than Bryce.

"He's nice," I say. "And it will be fun, and besides . . . it's my birthday. The birthday girl gets to do what she wants."

"No, Sela," she says adamantly. "I don't want to get in trouble, and you shouldn't go off with strangers. It's dangerous."

Something deep in my brain acknowledges the truth of this statement, but I push it aside. I'm sixteen, a hot guy is interested in me, and I want to see what the night holds. I'm feeling adventurous and a little vindictive, imagining having fun on my birthday with Dallas and relishing in being able to show up at some function in the near future with him on my arm and Bryce being jealous.

"I'm going," I tell Whitney resolutely. "And I really wish you'd come."

"Sela, don't," she implores me.

Turning away from her, I tell Dallas, "I have to be home by midnight. I live in Belle Haven."

"Not a problem," he says with a charming grin, and it wouldn't be. It's only a few miles away, and if worse came to worst, I could always cab it. I had the cash that Mom and Dad gave me for my birthday celebration with Whitney and so far, we'd only bought an ice cream tonight.

"Last chance," I say resolutely to Whitney with my head tilted to the side.

"This is not a good idea," she warns me, but my decision is made. Impulsively, I reach out and hug her. "I'll be fine."

She gives me a wan smile but it doesn't really project. She's worried and miffed I'm doing this, but I'm too filled with excitement to even care at this point. I turn toward Dallas and I'm beyond giddy when he takes my hand in his.

"Come on, gorgeous," he says as we start to walk away. "This will be a night to remember."

I totally know it will. Grandiose ideas fill my head of Dallas coming by my school to see me; maybe taking me to the spring dance. I swear I won't strut too much as we walk by Bryce and his mouth hangs open in disbelief. I look over my shoulder to see Whitney chewing on her bottom lip with worry, and I wave. She doesn't return it.

We all exit the mall to the upper-level parking garage, Dallas holding my hand while David and Blake walk ahead of us. They lead us over to a later-model Nissan that's got dark tinted windows, multiple stickers on the bumper, and a huge dent in the rear quarter panel. Blake takes the driver's door, David the front passenger, and Dallas and I crawl into the backseat.

"So, this party is supposed to be in some mansion or some shit; mostly college kids, but no one will say shit to us," Dallas tells me. "We're all eighteen."

Not me, I think, but I'm not about to tell him that. He doesn't ask, and I'm thankful.

Blake starts the car and a rap song I don't recognize comes on.

David drums his hands on the dashboard in quick succession and yells, "Yeah . . . spark that owl."

Dallas laughs and pops his hand on the back of David's headrest. "Hand me a stick, man."

I'm lost already, no clue what they're talking about. David reaches into the glove compartment, pulls something out, and hands it over his head to Dallas.

He takes it, reaches into his front pocket, and pulls out a lighter. Then he puts a thin white joint to his mouth and lights it. I stare in fascination as his cheeks hollow and the cherry on the end glows bright. It's not the first joint I've seen, because hell, the kids in my neighborhood stroll around in broad daylight smoking them, but it is the first time I've been in such close proximity.

Dallas holds the smoke in his lungs and exhales slowly, before passing it over to me with a wink. "Want a hit?"

I know I should pay attention to the warning bells going off inside my head, and the small tingle of fear in my belly, but then I *think of Bryce calling me a kid and I know without a doubt I don't want to be viewed that way.*

Besides . . . it's my sixteenth birthday and I deserve to have some fun. "You'll get me home by midnight, right?"

"Absolutely," *he says with a broad grin.*

I can't help it as I smile back, I take the joint from his hand, and bring it to my lips.

PRESENT TIME . . .

"That will be fifty dollars," the cab driver says, jolting me out of my memories. I turn my head to the right and see the familiar gray house of my childhood.

I pull my one and only credit card out of my wallet and swipe it through the digital reader attached to the seat in front of me. I wait for it to process and add a 15 percent tip, realizing that for the first time in forever I can use my card without worrying that it's going to max out.

Thanks, Beck. I really appreciate all the money you've given me to pay for school. It means I can actually afford things like a long cab ride out to Belle Haven.

I thank the cabbie and exit the vehicle, trudging up the sidewalk. I'm weary and I'm sad and this is the only place I thought to come. My apartment is foreign to me, having left that life firmly behind when I committed to moving in with Beck. It didn't seem right to go there, and all I could think about was crawling into my bed and sleeping away my misery.

Tomorrow I'd look at things with a fresh eye and a clear heart, and figure out where to go from there. I suppose I'd need to go back to my apartment, and hope that Beck will quickly deliver my clothes so I can have something to wear. I also need my phone, and I have class tomorrow at one P.M., but I'm thinking of skipping. Right now my heart isn't into anything except sleep.

I pull my keys out, locate the one I need, and open the door. Dad and Maria are both at work, and I'm glad. I don't think I can handle the questions that would inevitably come as to why I was showing up out of the blue in the middle of the day. I'll deal with them when they get home.

For now, I drop my purse onto the small side table beside the couch, dumping my keys inside. I walk back to my bedroom, which really doesn't look like my bedroom anymore. It still has my bed and dresser, but nothing left of the high school girl who once lived here. Maria's sewing machine sits on my old desk where I used to write in my journal.

I toe off my shoes and pull the covers back on the bed. I crawl in, pull them up over my head, and close my eyes. I try not to think of Beck, but that's virtually impossible. He was so many things to me in such a short period of time. He was a new life.

A fresh start.

A possibility I thought I'd never have.

But right now, he's the man who just broke me.

. . . .

CHAPTER 4

Beck

I pull up to William Halstead's house in Belle Haven, put the car in park, and cut the ignition. My pulse is hammering, my throat is dry, and my palms are sweating.

That's because Sela's in that house and I have no clue if I can fix what I just so carelessly broke several hours ago.

I've been going out of my mind all day with worry about her. I went to her apartment and I waited.

For three hours.

She never showed.

I went back to the condo, hoping she'd come there.

She never came.

At my wit's end, I dialed information and got the home number for William Halstead. Thank fuck he had a landline in a day and age when most people only had cell phones. I called three times, hanging up each time the answering machine came on. He finally answered an hour ago.

"Hello," he'd said in a booming voice.

"William . . . it's Beck North," I feel compelled to identify myself because even though we've met that one time before, he probably wouldn't recognize my voice.

"Beck . . . nice to hear from you," he said jovially, and by the tone of his voice I could tell Sela wasn't there. He'd never greet me so nicely otherwise.

"Listen . . . I'm looking for Sela," I told him, not wanting to beat around the bush. "We had a fight. A bad one, and I can't find her."

"I just walked in, but she's not here," he said, his tone going from amiable to worried. "When did you last see her?"

"Around ten thirty this morning."

"Did you try calling—" he started to ask, but then said, "Wait a minute. Her purse is on the table."

I held my breath and couldn't hear anything. Several seconds passed, and then he was back on the line, his tone low. "She's in her room . . . sleeping. What's going on?"

"I'm on my way there," I told him, ignoring his question.

"Beck," William said with worry. "What's going on?"

"That's for Sela to tell you, not me. But I'll be there in less than an hour." I cannot tell him how that clusterfuck went down, because I have no clue if he knows his daughter was raped. That's not my place to tell him that.

Silence, then a soft sigh. "Okay. See you soon."

I hung up, ran out of my condo, and hightailed it down to the garage. Rush hour was winding down but it was hell getting out of San Francisco.

And despite the fact I just had an hour to try to perfect my apology, I was as lost as I've ever been in my life. I have no clue how to make up for the fact that I was a supreme douche, and that I pretty much called her a liar about her rape. I can only hope that Sela has a forgiving heart and she lets me try to make it up to her, because I don't know what I'll do if I can't have her in my life.

My progress is slow as I make my way up to the house. William has apparently been watching out for me, because he opens the front door and steps out onto the porch, his hands tucked into his pockets. I stop at the end of the walkway and look up at him.

"Is she okay?" I ask hesitantly.

"No clue," William says, pinning me with a hard look. "I woke her up after you called. I told her you were coming but she's stayed in her room. I'm giving her space."

"I can't give her space right now," I tell him firmly. No fucking way am I leaving without talking to her.

"I'm not sure it's a good idea—"

"William." I cut him off. "I was here just three days ago, eating dinner in your house. You told me that Sela sometimes withdraws into herself. You told me if I ever caught her doing that, I had to pull her right back out again. So that's exactly what I'm going to do."

"She can be fragile sometimes," he says softly.

"That's not something I respected about her today," I tell him with bruising honesty. Sela may want her dad to know exactly what went down and I'm prepared for this bear of a man to try to whip my ass for it. "But I swear to you, I understand that now and I'm going to treat her with the care she deserves. I just need to talk to her."

"Did you hurt her?" His voice is hoarse and pained.

"Badly," I admit.

William's eyes get wet and his gaze slides away from me and out to the street. He swallows hard, takes a deep breath, and looks back at me. "Sela's had immense suffering in her life. She's—"

"I know," I tell him, because by those words it's clear to me that William Halstead knows his daughter was raped and he's suffered for it as well.

"You know?" he asks with surprise.

"Yes, and I handled it badly. I hurt her badly. So I'm begging you, William . . . please let me go in there and beg her forgiveness. Let me show her I can be a good man. Let me take responsibility for my wrongs and give me the chance to make it right for her. At the least, she deserves to know how very sorry I am."

He raises a meaty hand and scrubs his fingers through his hair, scratches at the back of his neck in contemplation. Finally, he nods and steps to the side of the porch, giving me silent permission to enter.

I expect him to snarl words of warning, or threaten to throw me out if I upset her, but he merely says ever so quietly, "Please make it right for her."

"I will," I say confidently, even though I'm scared shitless that I'll never see Sela look at me again with warmth, care, or desire.

The house is quiet when I walk in and I assume Maria's not here. I walk back to Sela's room and don't bother to knock on the door. I twist the knob and slowly open it, peering into the gloom. The lights are off, and the only way I can see Sela's bed is from an outdoor light that's on right outside of her room and illuminating the front yard. The glow filters in through the open blinds and I can see Sela laying on the bed, on her side, curled into a ball. My heart squeezes in pain over her attempt to crawl into herself.

There's enough ambient light that I make my way over to the side of her bed, reaching out to turn on the small lamp on her desk as I walk by it. My gaze locks on her and I'm surprised to find her staring straight at me, her blue eyes flat and empty.

Three more steps and I'm beside the bed. I kneel down on the carpeted floor, restraining myself from reaching out to her. Her face is blank, not a drop of emotion showing, but her eyes are slightly red, which tells me she's been crying.

I take a breath, let it out, and tell her, "You were raped by JT."

It's an emphatic statement. Not a question, not a guess, not a possibility. It's fact. It's truth.

So I acknowledge it.

She doesn't respond, but I don't want her to. I have so much more to say and I'm afraid her next words may very well be to tell me to get out.

So I press on. "It took only moments after I slammed that door in your face for it to sink in. Penetrate the truth of what you were saying. For me to believe you unequivocally. But you were already gone."

Another breath, and I quickly press forward, needing to explain my bad behavior before I could request absolution.

"Sela . . . you don't know much about my past, and if you give me the chance, I want to tell you all about it, but just know this . . . I couldn't even focus on what you were saying to me. It's like your words weren't punching through the anger, and I'm so fucking sorry for how much anger there was. My past has shaped me, and one of my weaknesses is a lack of tolerance for dishonesty. I couldn't see past you being in my office. I reacted so badly, and I'm ashamed and sickened of what I did to you. I have no excuse though . . . not really. I should have given you time to explain. I should have trusted there was an explanation. And when you told me that JT raped you, it truly just didn't seem possible to me. I thought you were talking about since you and I had met, and I just knew that wasn't the case. Knew it in my gut. But then quickly, I started thinking about everything I knew about you, and I remembered how you looked at JT that day you walked up to him at that Sugar Bowl Mixer. That look on your face. You hated him, and I realized . . . you *had* been raped by him. It had just happened long before you and I ever met, right?"

I don't wait for her confirmation, but I do lean forward a little closer to her as she stares at me. I don't think she's even blinked once during my story.

"I ran out of the condo after you, not five fucking minutes after you left. I couldn't find you. I went to your apartment and waited forever. I went back to the condo, hoping like hell you'd come back. I finally tracked you down here, and I had to come and tell you how very sorry I am for acting so harshly and not believing you. You have to know I'm going to beg your forgiveness after we talk, but please know this . . . I'll never forgive myself for what I did. I care about you so—"

"How did you know in your gut?" she asks softly, her first words to me, and I almost shudder in relief just from hearing her sweet voice. It's like music to my ears.

"Know in my gut?" I ask, confused.

"You said you knew in your gut I couldn't have been raped by JT since we'd met."

I hold nothing back, because if Sela grants me with her grace and forgives me, there aren't going to be any fucking secrets between us. "Caroline was raped," I say softly, and she gasps in response.

"Oh no," she says, sitting up slightly and leaning on her arm to peer at me. "Caroline?"

I nod, my heart twisting over the shit my sister's been through. "I've seen the hell a woman goes through right after. You weren't going through that, so I finally figured out . . . he had to have raped you a long time ago. Not to say you don't continually live with it day in and day out, but I've also seen how the healing can occur, and how you can move on with life. You clearly were doing that too. With me. It just finally made sense that you were talking about sometime in the past with JT."

She gives a tiny nod and drops her gaze from mine, her fingers plucking absently at the sheet. "It was ten years ago."

"I am so sorry, baby," I say, and I bring my hands to rest on the edge of the mattress. My voice cracks, almost deserts me, when I say, "I'm so fucking sorry, Sela. I can't stand to know you were hurt like that. It's tearing me up and I want to do something to make you feel better, but I don't know what to do other than beg you to let me try."

She drops her gaze again, her brows furrowing inward with consternation. For a moment, I know what I did was so heinous I feel like she just starts to slip away from me, but then her eyes snap back up to mine in question. "Do you really believe me?"

"That JT raped you?" I ask, but I know that's what she wants to know. "Yes. I absolutely believe you and I'm so fucking sorry that I wasn't telling you that immediately when you said it. I was just so angry about finding you in my office."

"But I was in your office. I stole your key, made a copy, and was searching through your office," she says with a pointed look.

"You forgive me Sela for what I did and you get a fucking pass on my office. In fact, you can look through anything in there you want."

And Christ above answering my prayers, she smiles at me. It's small and quite thin, but it's genuine.

She pushes up further on her arm, leans in toward me. "You hurt me."

"Yes," I whisper, my breath now frozen in my lungs as I await her verdict.

"Don't do it again."

"Never," I vow.

"It's actually a good thing," she says softly, and her hand slides across the bed to rest on mine. "That you hurt me."

I blink at her in surprise, my wrist turning so I can clutch her fingers. "Excuse me?"

"For me to be hurt like that, it means I cared for you deeply, otherwise your reaction wouldn't have mattered to me."

I grip her her tighter, almost afraid to hope.

"And for you to be so angry," she continues. "To the point where you weren't even really understanding what I was trying to tell you . . . Well, I guess that speaks to the same thing. You had feelings for me you felt were betrayed."

"Yes, but that's no excuse for—"

"Beck," Sela cuts me off, leaning closer to me. She rests her forehead on mine before whispering, "I'm tired, and I'd really like to go home to our condo."

"Thank fuck," I mutter before surging up and onto the mattress, pulling her hard into my arms. She presses her face into my chest, her arms wrapping around me, and I feel like I can finally breathe for the first time in hours.

. . . .

CHAPTER 5

Sela

The ride back to San Francisco is quiet but there's no tension. I don't have the stamina to hold on to it, and I don't have the strength to consider what's happened today. Beck holds my hand tightly, still expertly navigating his Audi through the darkness. Rush hour is over and the ride into the city goes by quickly.

Despite what I did to him today. Despite what he did to me. Despite what he's learned, despite the pain we've both caused, the silence is comfortable and unassuming. I know we have to talk, and I know he needs details. But God . . . I dread giving him the details. I know deep down the only reason Beck appears so calm right now is because he's in shock over what he's learned today, and I suspect still mired in guilt for the way he treated me. When he learns the whole truth of what happened to me . . . when he gets those terrible, sordid details . . . he's going to go ballistic. I just know it.

I need details too, because Beck's seen the devastation that rape can cause a woman. He's lived through it with Caroline, and despite the ache I constantly carry around due solely to that one hideous night of my life, my thoughts keep coming back to Caroline and the horror that she shares with me. I tried a survivor's therapy group about six months after my first hospitalization, and by the third session, I knew it wasn't for me. I didn't want to share what happened to me, and I didn't want to know what happened to the other women. Much of that had to do with the fact that I really didn't know what happened to me.

I had flash memories that I didn't realize were memories, but rather suspected they were nightmares. Vivid splashes of images and feelings that I thought were nothing more than my mind playing horrid tricks on me. The doctors explained that Rohypnol, in addition to relaxing me to the point where I wouldn't have been able to fight my attackers, causes partial amnesia. I existed in a world where I couldn't separate fact from fiction. It meant that I could give precious little in the way of valid information to the police to help them pursue my attackers.

I had no clue where Dallas and his friends had taken me, so the police couldn't investigate. I was too high to pay attention. I didn't even know Dallas and his friends' full names, no clue where they were from, or how the police could locate them. I had very little memory I could provide about what happened before I was given a drink laced with a date rape drug called Rohypnol, and that was due to the sole fact that I was stoned out of my mind when we arrived at the party. It was tremendously embarrassing to admit those things to the officers while my parents listened. They never showed an ounce of disappointment in me, which was a blessing, because the weight of my own self-hatred for putting myself in that situation was crippling.

So I had just tiny clips of moving images, almost like I was watching a movie in bed while on the verge of going to sleep. Not sure what I was seeing, not sure if I had seen it before, and completely clueless about whether it really happened at all. The only solid proof the police had that I had been raped was the blood in my underwear, the tears and bruises in my most private places, and the semen in my hair. Obviously, there was no match to the DNA in any criminal database, which meant my attackers didn't have criminal records.

So the case was dropped for lack of evidence, and I was left to rebuild my life around a crime that would never be solved.

Beck pulls into the garage of the Millennium Tower and inches into his reserved space. He opens my door and takes my hand to help me out of the passenger seat. His touch is warm, dry, and comforting as we make our way up to the penthouse.

The minute we step inside, I have an immediate burst of relief mixed with a touch of uncertainty.

I mean . . . where do we even go from here?

But Beck is Beck, and he takes charge. I suspect this is due to his experience in handling Caroline, and while the crimes against me are not fresh, the memories of them tonight are.

He pulls me down the hallway to our bedroom, right into the bathroom. Releasing my hand, he kneels beside the large garden tub and starts to fill it with hot water. He opens a bottle of my bubble bath and pours in a generous amount. I tuck my hands into my pockets, watching him test the heat of the water and make adjustments before standing up and wiping his hands on a towel.

Turning to me, he places his hands on my cheeks and leans in to kiss my forehead. "I suspect you'll tell me you're not hungry, but I'm going to make some soup for you all the same. And some tea. Get in the bath, take your time, and just relax."

I nod, because that sounds nice and it also gives me time to prepare for the inevitable talk I know we need to have. My hands go to the navy blue sweater I'm wearing, pulling it up and over my head. Beck watches me for a minute, his eyes warm and tender, but completely lacking in desire. This comforts me for the moment, and I drop the sweater to the marble floor.

Beck turns, walks back into the bedroom, and within a few moments, he's back again. He places one of his folded white T-shirts on the vanity with a pair of my panties on top. Turning to the back of the door, he pulls his robe off the hook and lays it at the foot of the tub. Another kiss to my temple while his hand wraps around the back of my neck, and he turns to leave.

"Beck?" I say quietly.

"Yeah, baby," he returns softly.

"I'm going to tell you everything."

"I'm ready to hear it when you're ready to tell it." His eyes are sad but reassuring. "I'll help you. I can't make it right, but I'll make it better. I promise. And I have things I need to tell you too."

I wonder if he'd help me kill JT. I wonder exactly how strong his loyalty will be to me.

I wonder exactly how in the hell he'll be able to look JT in the face tomorrow at work.

"Now get in the bath. I'll come check on you in a bit," he instructs me.

"Okay," I whisper, and watch as he gives me one more sad smile and walks out of the bathroom.

My eyes open, blinking against the harsh morning light streaming in through the wall of windows to my left. I rub my eyes, try to clear the fuzziness from my head left over from an incredibly exhausting day yesterday, and turn my head to the right. Beck's side of the bed is empty and the covers are pushed to the side. There's an indentation in his pillows, so it appears he slept here last night, although I don't have any recollection.

Then it comes back to me.

My bath.

Eating about half a bowl of soup before pushing it away.

Drinking the cup of chamomile tea he had prepared for me.

Taking my hand . . . pulling me up from the dining table.

Leading me to our bed and pulling back the covers.

Crawling in behind me, still wearing jeans and a white T-shirt, his lavender button-down discarded. "Let me just hold you. We can talk when you're ready."

My eyes closing and then . . . bright morning sunlight.

Sitting up, I push the sheet and blanket off me, swing my legs to the side, and stand up. I stretch, feeling well rested and strangely at peace for the moment. It's almost as if the events of yesterday created a massive purge of emotion in my system; the releasing of a huge and terrible secret to Beck; his acceptance and support. He doesn't know a single detail of what happened to me. He has no clue about the holes in my memory, or my murderous revenge plot. He's known me for all of a month and caught me breaking into his office, and yet he accepted my word about his partner and friend raping me. Beck brought me home last night, bathed and fed me, and then let me fall asleep in his arms.

Yes, I feel strangely at peace with absolutely no agenda for where I go next other than to find Beck and tell him my full story.

I use the bathroom, wash my hands, and brush my teeth. I pull my hair up into a ponytail and consider putting on a pair of sweatpants, but then dismiss the idea. I don't forget the fact that Beck crawled into bed with me last night fully dressed, something that he's never done before. He was handling me with care, treating me like a fragile glass bowl. My heart aches with the memory of what he told me last night.

Caroline was raped.

He's been through this, and right now, after the harsh realities of everything that happened yesterday, he's not quite sure how to handle intimacy with me. While the past twenty-four hours have dredged up some painful shit for both of us, it hasn't changed my want or desire for him. Beck suddenly knowing I was raped doesn't make me protective of my body. I gave that to him with no boundaries the minute we dispensed with condoms, and I'm not willing to give that up now that I've found it. I'm also not willing for him to have doubts or insecurities about my abilities to engage with some deep, no-holds-barred fucking the way we have been doing quite nicely.

So I leave the sweatpants behind and pad out of the bedroom in his white T-shirt that smells just like Beck, and my matching white panties.

My eyes hit the kitchen as I reach the end of the hallway but it's empty. They slide left taking in an empty couch, before finally landing on Beck, who is sitting on the floor, his back up against the eastern window. He's still dressed in his jeans and T-shirt, his bare feet planted on the wood flooring and his knees raised. His arms are looped around his shins and he stares back at me with warm eyes.

"Morning," he says quietly.

"Good morning," I say, my voice still a little rough with heavy sleep. "What are you doing?"

"Just waiting for you to get up. Figured you needed the sleep."

"How long have you been up?"

Beck raises his arm, twists his wrist to look at his watch. "A few hours."

My gaze goes to the mahogany and silver pendulum mantel clock over the fireplace and I see it's just past seven A.M. I look back at Beck and see his face is haggard, his eyes red with lack of sleep. He looks wary.

He looks scared.

He also sees me taking this all in and his face morphs into a tender smile as he pushes up off the floor. Immediately, he's removed the vulnerability I just witnessed, a brief moment where I now know that he's taken the weight of my problems onto his shoulders because he cares for me.

"Let's make you some tea," he says almost brusquely. He walks over to me, places his hands on my shoulders, and gives me a chaste kiss on my cheek.

Beck starts to pull away, but my hands shoot out, grasp on the backs of his arms, and I hold him in place. I raise up on tiptoes and place my lips to his. His breath blows out almost in a shudder and I press against him, open my mouth so his opens, and I give him a penetrating kiss.

A soft groan rumbles in his chest, and his tongue slips in my mouth as his arms drop to circle my waist. He pulls me in so our bodies are melded, angles his head, and deepens the connection. My heart soars that he accepts what I'm offering, and I'm content to let his mouth move against mine for a few intimate moments.

We mutually break and he brings one hand to my cheek. "You sleep okay?"

"Yeah," I say softly. "I'm good."

He smiles, takes my hand, and leads me into the kitchen. I lean up against the counter while he puts the kettle on to boil. He doesn't bother with coffee for himself, and I know he's already had his one cup for the day as evidenced by the empty mug in the sink. I watch him in silence, admiring the way his T-shirt pulls across the muscles of his back, his trim waist, and his fantastic ass in his jeans. I flush with desire, which seems more pervasive and consuming than it ever has before. I think this may be because Beck and I are very different to each other this very morning. Right now, he knows almost everything, and he didn't run.

He took care of me and continues to do so right now as he makes my tea.

When he has it prepared with just a small splash of skim milk, he turns and hands it to me. "What do you want to do today?"

It's a given he's not going in to work. I know he's not going to leave my side until he fully understands everything about me, why I came into his life, and what my agenda is. I also know, deep down, he's not prepared to handle what the fallout will mean as far as JT is concerned. I expect Beck's emotions are going to be bubbling with unexpressed fury by the time I'm done, and I brace myself that I'll need to control him so he doesn't act out rashly.

I know enough about Beck to know his relationship with JT is over, and I'm worried about the fallout regarding The Sugar Bowl. While bringing JT down is still on my agenda, I also feel an overwhelming need to make sure Beck is protected when it all shakes out.

"We should talk," I tell him before blowing on my tea to cool it.

"Yeah," he says quietly. "I need to know everything."

CHAPTER 6

. . . .

Beck

I need to know everything. Every last sordid detail so I can truly understand Sela and there will be no more walls and secrets between us. I need to hear the absolute truth, and then I need to move quickly to make things right.

Still, my stomach rolls with anxiety, as I know what I'm getting ready to hear is probably going to destroy me. The pain I bore for Caroline was different. I was her rock . . . the pillar of strength she used to get through her ordeal.

Sela's done most of that without me. While it's obvious she has an agenda with regard to JT, shit got ripped open wide yesterday and I know she's hurting again. Not only because of what happened to her, but mostly because of the callous way in which I handled it.

Turning from me, Sela walks into the living room. She puts her cup of tea on the coffee table and sits on one end of the white suede couch, curling her feet up underneath her. Legs bare, her breasts outlined against my T-shirt that dips low from the V-cut, she looks stunningly sexy. Yet I feel terrible for looking at her that way. I have no right, really.

Not right at this moment.

I follow her into the living room and she watches me as I round the couch. But rather than sit next to her, or even on the opposite end, I walk over to the window again. Tucking my hands into my pockets, I stare out over the bay, and I find comfort in the distance, which is odd, I know.

My internal instincts push me to walk over, pick Sela up, and settle her on my lap. I want to wrap my arms around her, open my ears, and let her pour her heart out in the safety of my embrace.

Yet I need these few feet between us complete with a coffee table barrier. Because although I want to wrap myself around her so she knows she'll never get hurt again, I've also got a rumbling vibration of violence settling deep in the pit of my stomach now that I know she's getting ready to lay it all out.

I turn my head over my shoulder and look at her. She smiles at me in understanding, leans forward, and pulls her cup of tea into her hands. When she curls it in toward her chest to hold the warmth against her, she murmurs, "Where do you want me to start?"

My heart cramps as I turn to face her fully. I rock up onto my toes, rock backward in a move of nervous energy. "From the beginning, I guess."

Sela takes a sip, looking abnormally composed. She leans forward, sets the tea on the table, and leans back against the cushions. With her hands folded in her lap, she tilts her chin up and says, "I was sixteen. It was my birthday."

My breath rushes out between my teeth, making a hissing sound. Her eyes soften and she gives me a knowing smile.

She fucking smiles at *me* to give *me* comfort.

My heart squeezes again, and I almost take a step toward her, but her next words stop me dead in my tracks.

"It was my fault, really."

"No fucking way," I snarl, my hands coming out of my pockets and clenching into fists.

She holds her hand up, palm out to me in a sign of quiet. My mouth snaps shut.

"Just listen," she whispers.

I force my hands to unclench, and so they don't do it again, I hook my thumbs in my pockets and lock my knees for stability.

"My boyfriend had just broken up with me the day before. He was a few years older and thought I was just a kid. I was hurt, as only a sixteen-year-old could be who had all kinds of silly, romantic notions in her head and was eager to prove herself as a woman."

I can't stand it. Laying this . . . this . . . blame on herself. I turn slightly from her and take a few paces while she talks.

"I went to the mall with my best friend the night of my birthday. Met a cute boy."

"JT?" I can't help the growl coming out of my mouth as I pivot, pace a few steps the other way as I stare at her.

She drops her gaze to her lap and shakes her head with a wry smile. "No. Just a cute boy that I foolishly thought would be just the ticket I needed to prove that I was worthy of notice. I left my bestie behind and went with him and some friends to a party. We got stoned on the way there. My first time ever smoking pot, and I was out of it. Had no clue where they even took me, but it was a huge mansion and it was the most amazing thing I'd ever seen. Filled with young people, mostly college students. I had a cute boy with his arm around my shoulder, I was stoned out of my mind, and laughing my ass off. I thought it was the best thing ever."

I halt because her last words have an ominous ring to them.

"What happened?"

She lifts her eyes to mine. "The cute boy found a prettier girl than me, and soon I was left all alone. That pissed me off, hurt my feelings. Made me feel terrible and lonely. I thought about leaving, but then . . ."

Sela hesitates, gives a slight cough, and continues with more strength in her voice. "But then I had the attention of another cute boy. Older. College age, I guess. He flirted with me, told me how beautiful I was. Talked about college and frat parties, and hinted that maybe we could go out together. So I turned the flirting charm back onto him. I batted my eyes, stuck my chest out, did whatever I could to prove that I could hang with an older crowd. That I was mature and worldly, and it was so stupid, but I even thought . . . screw the boy I'd come with. He was just a boy. This was a man. A college guy that was interested in me. I even thought about how he'd take me to spring dance, and my ex-boyfriend would be so jealous. I let him kiss me, and rub his hand on my ass. I pressed into him, and although I really didn't know what I was doing, he liked it and it made me bolder."

"Not your fault," I whisper hoarsely, and she gives me an accommodating nod.

"Maybe not," she whispers back. Another clearing of her throat, and her voice is strong again. "At any rate, I don't know how much time passed. I was given beer. We hung out. We danced. I was having the time of my life and all I could keep thinking was that this was the best birthday ever."

She stops, her story hitting a wall. Her gaze drops back to her lap and her fingers work in a nervous twining around each other. I wait her out, knowing that she's getting to the horror part of her story, and I swallow against the bile building up in my throat.

When she finally looks at me again, her eyebrows are drawn inward in frustration. "Then I don't remember much of anything. Bits and pieces. Tiny flashes of images, sounds, smells."

"I don't need details," I tell her softly. Begging her, perhaps, not to tell me the details.

"But you do," she argues simply, and doesn't give me room to argue back. "There were three of them. I can't remember a lot, but I'm sure there were three."

"Sela," I whisper. A simple statement of remorse and pain that three men violated her. This was worse than I ever could have imagined.

She pins me with a direct stare, her chin coming up higher in a pose of absolute defiance of the horror that befell her. "The first one took my virginity. I was so out of it I don't even think I felt pain, but I remember him grunting on top of me. The next one wanted me to suck his dick, but was afraid I'd bite him, so he raped my ass."

"No," I wheeze out, the air burning my chest as it's expelled.

Her chin goes higher. "Then JT was on me while someone else held me down. I remember panties stuffed in my mouth so I couldn't scream, but honestly . . . I didn't have the strength to. I just laid there . . . and took it."

I hunch over, hands to my knees, and stare at the floor as I swallow hard . . . willing myself not to scream or throw up.

"I only have flashes . . . snippets of scenes. He pulled out of me, removed the panties, and came in my mouth. Put his hand over my nose and mouth and made me swallow it. That is one of the clearer memories."

I lurch upward, the room spinning and my vision going dark for a moment until I become focused on the front door to the condo. I bolt toward it, snarling, "I'm going to fucking kill him. Going to beat him to a bloody pulp."

Sela flies off the couch and steps in my way, hands coming firmly to my chest. I look down at her, see the strength and resistance in her eyes, and my hands clap to her wrists. Not in an effort to push her away, but with burning need to pull her into me. My arms wrap around her upper back and I hunch my shoulders so I come protectively around her.

"I'm going to kill him," I whisper, my throat burning and tears stinging my eyes.

"No, you're not," she says softly, her own hands moving to my lower back and pressing in. She rubs slow circles, willing me to calm down. But all I can imagine is my fists pummeling into JT's face, until his nose breaks, then smashes, then becomes obliterated until he starts to drown in his own blood. I'm going to hold my hand over his nose and mouth and I'm not going to let up until his lungs suffocate with blood.

"Calm down," she murmurs, rubbing harder at my back. "You need to hear it all."

"I can't," I croak out, sniffing in deeply and blinking my eyes to clear the wetness.

Sela leans back, far enough so she can look up at me. "Let me get it all out, Beck. You haven't heard the worst."

"I can't," I implore her. Because it will only fuel me to come up with something even more heinous to rain down on JT's head.

"Please."

"Sela."

"Please, Beck," she says, then wraps a delicate hand around my wrist. She leads me to the couch, and my leaden legs don't move for a moment, so she pulls on me harder. I follow numbly and she pushes me down onto a cushion, crawling right onto my lap to straddle me. My arms encircle her lower back automatically, hers going to my shoulders as she looks down at me.

"Somehow I got home. JT put me in a cab, paid the driver, I suppose. I was out of it, not really sure what happened to me . . . just those flashes that I described to you. I was starting to feel pain; I had bruises starting to form and while I was still stoned and drugged, I had this sort of deep understanding that I had caused this to happen."

My body tightens but she continues, not letting me rebuke her for the blame game again.

"I got a utility knife out of the kitchen drawer. Went into the bathroom. I hated myself so much for what I'd let happen to me—for being stupid enough to even go with strangers to that party, for flirting and pretending to be a big girl—that I cut down into my left wrist."

I suck in a startled breath before grabbing on to her wrist, twisting it so I could see. I had seen it before, I realized. My thumb grazes over the small, inch-long scar that cuts at an inward angle. It's thin and red with a slightly raised and bumpy edge, but it's so small I never would have connected it with a desire to end one's life.

"I didn't try hard enough," she whispers, and I raise my eyes to hers. "I pressed down, and the minute it punched through my skin, I regretted it. There was a lot of blood, but it wasn't a large cut and I didn't hit a vein. I was still high as a kite and I fell to the floor, I think more wigged out over what I'd just done than anything. It woke my parents and they found me quickly. Called an ambulance."

"Christ," I mutter, looking back down at the scar.

She's silent, giving me a moment to collect myself. I consider everything she's told me. A brutal gang rape, the loss of her innocence, and a brief, desperate moment where she thought to end the pain forever. But the strength she must have had, to pull herself back from the brink before she could do irrevocable harm.

"No one realized I was raped until the doctor examined me. My parents were freaking out I had tried to kill myself, not having a clue about what really happened. They obviously tended to the wrist first, but once they realized what had happened to me, they used a rape kit. The police came and I was interviewed for what seemed like forever. They found Rohypnol in my system, which is why I don't remember much."

Still holding her wrist, stroking the scar, I ask, "I don't understand. This was ten years ago. Why wasn't JT arrested?"

"Because I didn't know who he was. Couldn't even remember much about my attackers other than vague features. Color of hair, maybe an idea of how tall they were. I didn't even know where the mansion was located. They tried to investigate as best they could. Contacted local cab companies to see if they could find who drove me to my house, but they couldn't come up with anything."

"Then how did you know it was JT?" I ask, not in a disbelieving way, because I trust fully that Sela knows he was involved.

Sela's hands move, dislodging my own so she can lace our fingers together. "I was hospitalized involuntarily because of my suicide attempt. It was a pitiful attempt, but it was enough to hold me. It was the first of three hospitalizations that happened over the next few years. I drove myself crazy trying to remember details. Drove myself to absolute breakdowns fueled by guilt and self-loathing for even putting myself in that situation. I barely graduated high school. Lost all my friends because I couldn't stand to have them looking at me, wondering what was going on inside my deranged mind. I became paranoid, worried I'd get attacked again, so I hardly ever went anywhere. My parents circled in closer, became almost obsessive in their protection of me. I tried counseling and group therapy, but none of it helped. It's like I kept filling up with all of these horrible feelings compounded with helplessness at not having resolution, until I'd just snap and get committed again, although I never tried to kill myself after that first attempt."

"How did you survive?" I ask her pleadingly, because I need her to get to the part where she tells me she pulled through.

She gives a shrug and a light laugh. "I just . . . gave up trying to figure it all out. Also, I took some really good antidepressants, but eventually I just had to move on. It helped when I enrolled in college, gave me a new focus."

"But there came a point when you figured it was JT?" I prompt her.

"Yes," she says with serious eyes. "A little over six months ago. I was watching an entertainment news show, and JT was on it. They were doing a piece about The Sugar Bowl."

"And you recognized him?" I guess.

Her eyes turn a darker shade of blue, her lips flatten out in a grimace. "No. I recognized the tattoo of the red phoenix on his rib cage. It was one of the things I distinctly remembered that night. One of the other guys had one on his wrist too."

This news jolts me so hard I come flying up off the couch, clutching Sela by the hips so she doesn't fall off. I quickly set her on the floor and take three steps to the side, away from her. My mouth hangs open in disbelief, and my left arm comes up across my chest, over my right shoulder, where my fingertips press into the area where the top of my phoenix tattoo resides.

She watches me carefully, knowing the impact this is having.

"I wasn't there," I croak out, thinking the reason she's watching me is to see if there's culpability.

Immediately, her eyes grow apologetic and she steps toward me quickly. I step backward but that doesn't stop her. She barrels into me, hands coming up to clasp to the sides of my head. She presses her fingers in and holds me tight. "I know you weren't. You couldn't. I know you, Beck, and I know you'd never do that to a woman."

"It's why you ran," I murmur. "The morning after we met.

You saw my tattoo . . . when I was in the shower. Didn't you? So you thought then that I might have."

"It was before I knew you, Beck," she chides me. "Yes, it freaked me out, but by the time you came to my apartment the next day, I had reasoned it out. There's no way a man who gave me my first orgasm . . . made me feel safe and secure enough to let go, could ever do that to me. I don't understand the connection with the tattoo, but I know it doesn't revolve around rape. I know it in my heart."

CHAPTER 7

. . . .

Sela

Beck pulls away from me, takes another step back, and his hand covers his mouth as he looks at me with wild eyes. He reminds me of a spooked animal, but I knew the tattoo connection was going to send him in a tailspin.

"You've done nothing wrong, Beck," I say softly, hoping to calm him down.

He lets out an almost hysterical bark of a laugh as his hand drops. "I kicked you out of our condo when you told me you were raped. I . . . I . . . took the side of a gang rapist over yours, and fucking threw you out in the hallway like a piece of trash."

"Easy, baby," I coo as I walk up to him. "You need to let that go."

"Fuck," he cries out in a deep bellow of misery as he looks at me with tortured eyes. "How could you even trust me? I'm a fucking friend and business partner to a rapist; I didn't believe you when you told me when JT—"

"You believe me now," I say firmly as I take one more step into his space and place my hands on his chest. "And you apologized for that crap that went down yesterday. You had reason to be pissed at me. I broke into your office, Beck. I betrayed your trust too, yet you've let that go. You have to trust that I can let it go too."

He drops his head with a loud sigh and curls one hand around the back of my neck. He tips his face until his forehead rests against mine. "I'm so fucking sorry this happened to you, Sela. I'll help make this right, I swear it. I'm going to make JT pay for what he did."

I don't say anything for a moment, letting Beck continue to take deep breaths while the gravity of everything he just learned settles in. Finally, he lifts his head slightly, grazes his lips against my forehead, and asks, "Why were you in my office?"

Taking him by the hand again, I lead him back over to the couch. I think he needs to be sitting for the rest of my story, because I know it's going to piss him off.

After a slight push, he sits back down, but rather than straddle his lap again, I sit my butt on the coffee table, directly across from him. Our knees brush against each other, a comforting touch. Still, I remain poised and alert for him to flip out on me again.

"When I learned that JT was one of my rapists, I became obsessed with revenge. I considered only briefly going to the police, but it didn't hold any appeal to me because I couldn't be sure my word would hold up against his. My memory was so riddled with holes, and I'm only reasonably certain of the pieces I do remember. You have to realize, for years I thought those flashes weren't even real. I thought they were just products of my imagination . . . nightmares so to speak. Because my memory was unreliable as evidence, I wasn't confident I could get justice, and besides . . . it would only be justice against JT. I wanted to know who the other two were."

"So you thought to confront him that night we met?" Beck asks with raised eyebrows. "Just thought you'd walk up, introduce yourself as the woman he raped, and he was going to admit to it?"

"No," I say softly, and resist the urge to drop my gaze. "I was going to get him alone and I was going to make him tell me while I pointed a gun at his face."

Beck's jaw drops.

"Then I was going to put a bullet in his brain," I say with deadly promise.

"You're fucking kidding me," he whispers in disbelief.

"I'm not," I assure him. "I was obsessed with it. I was going to torture him with the fear of dying, then I was going to rid the world of his evil. Then I was going to find the other two men and give them the same retribution."

"Sela," Beck admonishes, refusing to believe I could be so cold-blooded.

"Don't," I say sharply. "Don't judge me in a place you could never hope to stand. You can never begin to understand what those monsters did to me."

Beck shakes his head adamantly, leans forward, and places his hands on my thighs. "No, I'm not judging your intent or your desire. I want to kill him myself. But I can't let you do something that would stain your soul. Christ, you could get arrested for murder and get sent to prison."

"I know," I whisper. "And I changed my mind eventually. I decided to give up my quest."

"When?" he prompts.

"When I let you into my body without a condom," I murmur, and watch as his eyes go soft and tender. "When I gave my full trust to you. I knew that you were more important than my revenge, and I didn't want to lose it."

A low whistle of breath comes out of Beck's lips, but then he tilts his head to the side in confusion. "But then why were you in my office? You said it was about JT."

Now I drop my gaze, because this is the part I'm embarrassed to admit. If there is one stumbling block remaining between what Beck and I could have for a future, it's right here.

Placing my hands over his, I swallow hard and look back up at him. "That night we went to dinner with JT. I saw how happy you were. I knew all the shit he was handing you was nothing but shit. He was putting on an act, making you believe you chose wisely in a friend and partner. He was the total opposite with me in the limo. He belittled and taunted me. I saw the way you laughed and told stories and jokes with JT, knew it was a fucking act, and it pissed me off. While I think to some extent I logically knew that didn't change your feelings about me, it did renew my fury against him. I just . . . snapped. Suddenly, I wanted revenge again. I wanted him out of my life so I wouldn't have to suffer another fucking dinner and sit across from the table with your business partner—the man that raped me—while making polite conversation. I wanted him out of your life. I wanted to free you from his poison and then you'd have control of The Sugar Bowl, and then finally . . . finally, you and I could have the life we were meant to have. Together. So I decided to go through with my plan and I was looking in your office for anything that would help me accomplish it. I scored by getting his home address."

I finish with a shuddering breath, waiting to see what Beck will do. I don't know if he can understand just how easily I was swayed again toward revenge and murder, but I don't know if I will be able to handle it if he can't accept my weaknesses.

A look comes over Beck's face, one filled with anguish and fatigue. He pulls one hand out from under mine and scrubs it over his face. His eyes dart to the right and he takes a deep breath, and when they slide back my way, what he tells me next causes my world to tilt.

"Sela . . . JT is my brother."

"What?" I gasp in astonishment as I rear backward.

"It fucking kills me to even claim we share the same blood, but yeah . . . he's my brother. Half brother to be exact."

"I don't understand," I whisper, not able to even fathom this revelation. "I never read anything about that. You've never said anything."

"No one knows," he says bitterly. "JT doesn't even know. Only my father and his mother. And me, of course."

"I . . . I . . ." Fuck, I'm speechless.

Beck leans forward, places his hands on my shoulders. His face comes near mine and his eyes pin me in place. "I'm not telling you that to elicit any sympathy for his cause. The fact we share blood isn't going to save him from me. I'm going to make him pay, but you need to know why I really kept giving him chances. I'd all but given up on him as a friend and business partner. That blood tie was the last thin straw that was causing me to give him that one final chance. And yeah . . . I was fucking taken in by him at dinner that night. He snowed me, apparently, and knowing we share the same blood made it easier for me to fall into it. But not anymore. He's fucking dead to me and I swear I'm going to make him pay."

Warmth flushes through me over his heated vow. While I definitely want to know more about this blood tie he shares with JT, I'm more interested to know how complicit Beck will become in my plans. I have an avenging angel on my side now, and together we can rid JT from our existence.

"Will you help me kill him?" I whisper.

The blood drains from Beck's face, and now he's the one that jerks backward. "Christ, Sela. No, we can't fucking kill JT. We have to go to the police."

"But you said—"

He rolls right over me. "I said I'd make him pay. I might beat him senseless first, but then we're going to the police. He's going down for this but we're letting the legal system handle it."

I try to tamp down the rage that swelters hot within me and I push up from the coffee table until I'm standing over Beck on the couch. "He raped me with two of his buddies. Took away my innocence, held me down while some faceless monster tore my ass up, and then made fun of me when the jizz I didn't swallow was dried to a crust in my hair. He put me in a cab, without a care in the world that he'd be caught, and then he went back inside to party with his friends. I'm sure the only thought that man has given me in the past ten years is to jack off to the memory of what he did to me, and you don't think he deserves to die?"

"Yes, he deserves to die," Beck says with a hard edge to his voice. "But not at the risk of you getting caught."

"But we could come up with a plan—"

"For fuck's sake, Sela," Beck bellows as he stands up from the couch and gets in my face. He's furious, and for the first time during this discussion, it's at me and not himself or JT. "We cannot plot to murder someone. It won't work. We'll get caught."

I know he's right, and because he's right and killing my dream of revenge with his practicality, I get just as pissed, so I yell back at him, "Then just how in the hell are you going to make him pay, Beck? Huh? What grand scheme do you have that could possibly make up for what he did to me?"

"I don't know," he says tiredly, stepping to the side and around me. I turn my body, keeping my eyes on him as he paces over to the window. He shoves his hands back inside his pockets and his shoulders sag with the weight of what I just placed on him.

"I can't let it go," I tell him softly, and I hope he hears the resolve in my voice.

"Neither can I," he says as he stares out over the bay waters. "But I need time to think. To process all of this. I need to figure out how we can avenge you and let me keep The Sugar Bowl intact."

"Murder," I whisper, even though I know that's not the right answer. Despite wanting JT's blood on my hands—fuck, despite wanting to bathe in his blood—I know there's too much at risk. I know the chances of doing this cleanly and without suspicion are low. I also know that the real reason I know I can't do it is because if I were to get caught, I would lose Beck, and he's the most precious thing in my life. He's just more important than my wanting JT's head on a platter.

Beck doesn't answer me but he doesn't need to. I suspect his brain is on overdrive right now, trying to figure something out.

. . . .

CHAPTER 8

Beck

The complete truth is out, and now it's time to destroy JT.

Sela has two classes at Golden Gate this afternoon. I suggested she skip them because both of us are emotionally wrung out, and figured maybe we could go for a drive up the coast to continue to talk things out. I still had to tell her the details about JT's relation to me, and I assume she wants to know more about Caroline.

But Sela nixed my idea, adamantly insisting that while we clearly had things to decide and even more things to discuss, that she needed to keep her life normal as well. This ended up being for the best, because it forced me to jump onto the problem of figuring out how to bring JT down. Ideally, I'd like to go to the police and let them handle it. They have DNA, and according to Sela, it's JT's. But I don't know if her word and faulty memory would be enough to make them force a DNA test. And I don't want JT to know we're coming after him. I want to hit him when he doesn't have a chance in hell to protect himself.

After Sela left, I unlocked my office door and didn't have any intention of locking it again. While we may not see eye to eye on how to handle the situation with JT, I'm going to show her that I don't intend on there being secrets between us ever again.

Within moments, I had the appropriate folder pulled from my filing cabinet and I was online, logging into the secure server at The Sugar Bowl. A few keystrokes and I was staring at a photo and personal profile of Melissa Fraye, the Sugar Baby JT tried to drug a little over two weeks ago at the mixer. One more tap on my keyboard and I was staring at her phone number and home address. I jotted them down on a yellow sticky pad sitting on my desk and pulled the note off after standing from my desk. Another fifteen minutes to take a quick shower and put on fresh clothes, and I was on my way to visit Melissa Fraye.

I knock on the apartment door and take a step back so if Melissa is inside, she can see my face clearly through her peephole. I immediately hear footsteps on the other side of the door before it opens a few inches, secured with a chain.

A woman who is not Melissa Fraye peeks around the edge at me.

"Is Melissa here?" I ask her.

"Yeah, just a minute," she says before shutting the door on me, which doesn't bother me in the slightest. This isn't the best neighborhood, so it's not wise to open the door to strange men.

I wait patiently for a few minutes, then the door opens again, this time fully, and I'm looking at Melissa Fraye as she appraises me. Eyes sliding down, taking in my John Varvatos jeans, Tomas Maier T-shirt that probably cost more than her entire wardrobe, and my Aquatalia suede boots, there's no doubt she knows I'm wearing a fortune in designer clothes, and I know this because by the time her eyes reach me again, I can almost see dollar signs in them.

"Do you know who I am?" I ask.

She nods, cocks a hip, and presses it against the edge of the door. "Beckett North."

"I need to talk to you. Can I come in for a moment?"

"Of course," she says with a brilliant smile and a nervous flutter of her fingers through her hair. She's a pretty girl and all, but she doesn't have shit on Sela.

Melissa opens the door and steps aside to give me entrance. I immediately take in the small but clean apartment, decorated in mismatched, used furniture and cheap prints on the walls framed in acrylic. The woman who opened the door stands in the tiny kitchen, hunched over a gossip magazine, chewing gum heavily.

"We need privacy," I tell Melissa.

The dollar signs burn brighter and she says, "We can go in my room."

I don't argue with her. I don't care if we talk here or in her room, and I'm not worried about my virtue. I can handle her, but I do not need prying ears for what I'm about to discuss.

Melissa's room is messy, with clothes littered all around the floor. She makes a show of kicking a few pieces under her unmade bed as I shut the door behind me.

"Sorry about all this," she says as she bends to pick up a bra off the floor. She doesn't stuff this under the bed, but instead lays it on top where I guess she wants me to admire the large, pale blue lacy cups or something.

I don't give it another thought and get straight to the point. "I need to talk to you about the last Sugar Bowl Mixer you attended on the twenty-first."

Her head tilts at me in curiosity. "I was there. Having a drink with your partner as a matter of fact, but he bailed."

I nod. "Was that the first time you'd met JT?"

"Yeah," she said with a fond smile. "Never thought I'd get a shot at him, but he zeroed in on me pretty fast. I really thought something would come out of that, but like I said . . . he bailed."

I reach into my back pocket, pull out the copy of the agreement that JT said Melissa signed, and hand it to her. She opens it up, glances at it once, and then looks back up to me with confusion in her eyes.

"Is that your signature at the bottom?" I ask, nodding my head toward the paper in her hands.

She peers down at it, brows furrowed, and says, "It looks like it."

"Did you sign it?"

Her eyes start flying across the words of the agreement, all the while her brow furrowing deeper and deeper. Finally her eyes raise to mine and the dollar signs are gone. I see a flash of anger as she hands it back to me. "I didn't sign that. Nor would I ever do something like that."

I take the document from her, shove it back into my pocket. "I didn't think so."

My stomach churns with the realization that JT was going to rape this woman. He was going to drug her, the way he did Sela, and he was going to do with her whatever he pleased. Fuck, for all I know he's got an entire gang of buddies that rape with him, and I know at least one of them is in our fraternity, because Sela saw his tattoo.

"What's this about?" she asks suspiciously, her arms now crossing over her chest.

I had suspected she didn't sign this agreement. On the way over here, I had debated whether or not to tell her the truth of what almost happened to her. On just a quick consideration, it could have been a good play. No doubt she's pissed and I bet she'd want to report this to the police. A criminal investigation would ensue, but then I know what would happen. JT would offer to pay her off and I figure she'd take it and drop the charges.

So I lie to her, feeling only a slight bit of guilt, which I quickly push away by telling myself I saved her from getting raped. That should be good enough for now.

"It's a sick-as-fuck prank someone's trying to play on me," I tell her smoothly. "Nothing for you to worry about now that I confirmed you didn't sign this."

I expect her to question me further. At the very least, after what she read in that document, she should have some concern for her safety. Instead, she just nods and asks, "Would you, um . . . like to go out and get a drink or something?"

It takes every effort for me to put an engaging smile on my face. "Thank you, Melissa, for that offer. But I actually have somewhere I need to be."

"Well, maybe some other time," she says desperately as I turn toward her bedroom door.

"Maybe," I say, just to let her down easy. She's a cute girl. She'll find a real Sugar Daddy soon.

The minute I'm back in my car but before I turn the ignition, I flip through the contacts on my phone until I find what I'm looking for, and tap the screen to dial.

He answers on the second ring. "What's up, man?"

Robert Colling is a fraternity brother of mine, and while he doesn't sport a red phoenix tattoo, we were and still are pretty close. He went on to law school and now handles sleazy and messy divorces here in the Bay Area.

"Need a favor," I tell him as I start the car.

The Bluetooth engages and his reply comes over the speakers in my car. "Anything. Lay it on me."

"I need a recommendation for a good private investigator, and I'd like it to be one with a low moral compass. Not afraid to get his hands a bit dirty."

Robert whistles into the phone. "Damn, man . . . what do you have cookin'?"

"Can't say."

"Let's pretend I'm your attorney and privilege is invoked. You can tell me."

"Can't," I say resolutely, "but I'll buy you a beer sometime soon in payment."

"You suck," he says with a chuckle. "I'll text the information to you as soon as we hang up. I have the perfect guy for you. Highly trustworthy and will do anything you need for the right price."

"You're the best, man," I say.

"Just don't call me to bail you out of jail when whatever game plan you have goes south," he warns jokingly.

"I won't," I say, although he'd probably be the first person I'd call if I got arrested and needed bailing out.

I disconnect the call and toss the phone onto my passenger seat to wait for his text. Putting my Audi in gear, I check my right passenger mirror, and seeing the street is clear, pull away from the curb. Holding on to the wheel with my right hand, my left comes across my chest and over my shoulder, much the same way it did this morning, and I press my fingers down into the muscles below the top of my tattoo.

It's nothing more than a stupid membership inside the inner circle of my fraternity. During rush week, I was approached and offered admission by some of the upperclassmen, which ironically included JT. He was in his senior year while I was a freshman. All I had to do was a stupid prank they chose to prove my worthiness, and I was admitted. Certain benefits came with the admission, including a coveted room inside the fraternity house.

My prank was easy. All I had to do was spray paint some graffiti on the side of the dean's house. I chose a rival fraternity's letters, which my brothers all thought was hilarious. I got away scot-free, and after I was inducted into the frat, I got my tattoo the very next weekend.

But what if something more sinister had been required of the other members? Was Sela's rape part of an initiation? She said one other guy had the tattoo already on his wrist, but on the other guy she didn't see one. Doesn't mean he didn't have one, but what if he was a lowerclassman and his induction into our secret society was to participate in Sela's rape?

It's a distinct possibility, one that I didn't think had existed just a day ago. But now I don't put anything past JT. I could easily see him duping or enticing like-minded sociopaths to jump in on that plan of action, especially if everyone was high on booze and drugs.

Sela can't remember much about the other two men involved. One had dark hair, the other pale blond. That's it, and with only that as a description, I doubt I'm going to be able to identify them through fraternity records.

Still going to try to pull some possibilities though and see if they unclog her memory some more. That's one of the reasons I want a private investigator.

Speaking of which, my phone chimes with the familiar *whoop* sound of an incoming text. I pick it up from the passenger seat, and while flicking my eyes between the road and the screen, I navigate my way to the texts.

Robert sent just the PI's name and number.

I tap my thumb on the blue link of the phone number and the

Bluetooth connects the call. After a few rings, I get a recorded message:

This is Dennis Flaherty. Sorry I missed you. Leave your info and I'll get back to you soon.

After the beep, I say, "Yeah . . . Dennis . . . my name is Beck North. You were recommended to me by Robert Colling. I have a job I'd like to hire you for. It's urgent and it's big, and money is not an object. I'd like to meet with you today to discuss it."

I leave my number and disconnect, eager to have him call me back.

I think that before Sela and I can decide what to do about JT, we need to dig up every piece of dirt we can on him. I need to wade through the pile of scummy shit I'm sure he's been involved in and figure out what I can use to my benefit.

And there's no doubt . . . JT probably has a lot of dirty shit out there he's left behind, probably not a care in the world it would ever be used against him. In fact, I'm sure he's sitting in his office right now, probably surfing the Net, maybe planning his next rape, whatever.

The point being that I guarantee his ego would never let him consider the possibility that he can be taken down.

I cannot wait to prove him wrong about that.

CHAPTER 9

. . . .

Sela

I enter the condo and see Beck's keys on the foyer table, so I know he's home. I wasn't sure what he did today, but I know he didn't go into work. He'd said, *"Sela, I can't be in the same building with that scumbag. There's no telling what I'd do."*

I understand his sentiment exactly. It's how I felt that first time I came face-to-face with JT at the mixer when I still had murder as my number-one plot to get my vengeance. I remember the actual ache inside me after looking at his evil face, the almost desperate force of willpower not to pull my gun out and shoot him point-blank in front of two hundred witnesses.

Even without looking into the kitchen, I can sense Beck isn't in there.

Too quiet.

And I can see he's not in the living room.

So I drop my book bag on the floor and head toward our bedroom. As soon as I turn down the hallway, I see his office door open with light spilling out from the late-afternoon sun that's also shining through the living room windows overlooking the bay.

I walk softly, the navy blue suede ballet flats I had worn today falling much more silently than my squeaky tennis shoes. When I turn into his office doorway, I see Beck bent over his desk, one hand rubbing at the back of his neck while the index finger of the other hand skims over lines of a document as he reads it.

He senses my presence and looks up at me with a worn smile as I stand hesitantly in the doorway.

"Hey," he says as he leans back in his chair and stretches his arms above his head. He bends his neck side to side, loosening out kinks that indicate he's been hunched over that desk for quite a while.

"Hey," I say back.

"You can come inside, you know," he says with a quirk of his lips.

"Are you sure?" I tease back, happy that there seems to be not an ounce of lingering resentment that I broke into this place just yesterday.

Beck sweeps his hand toward the filing cabinet. "Dive in if you want. No secrets."

I chuckle and step into his office, walking around his desk and coming to a stop beside his chair. He swivels it to look at me. "School good today?"

"Yeah, all good," I say as I look down at the document on his desk.

"The Townsend-North operating agreement," Beck says with a grimace. He waves his hand at it. "Hell, you should read the damn thing. I've been over it ten times. My attorney's looked at it. Not a single damn thing in there that I can use to get him out."

I ignore the document. There's no sense in me reading it if Beck and his attorney have. Still, I have to ask, "Does he own the majority of the company?"

Beck shakes his head. "We're fifty-fifty. He contributed start-up capital, which he's already paid back from the first profits. I put in the technical expertise, and got paid an amount equal to his start-up capital. Now we divide everything in half. All major decisions have to be bilaterally approved by both of us."

"And has that always happened?"

"No. He's made a few bad investments without running it by me. But they were minor and ended up being good tax write-offs."

"So you can't use that?" I prod.

"Nope. Not good enough, but I'm meeting tomorrow with an investigator I'm going to hire to dig into JT's life. I just know that asshole has to have some dirty dealings. He's too amoral not to, and I'm hoping there's something we can use there."

I nod in understanding, a warm kernel of security starting to blossom deep in my chest. While I went off to school today and played at being a college student, Beck's been trying to figure out how to bring JT down. While my parents have always been my champions, I've never had another single person in my life care about me to that extent. It's actually quite humbling.

And a turn-on at the same time.

Last night I was dead to the world and Beck slept beside me in our bed fully clothed. He's not made a single move on me since we've been back, and there's been opportunity. There was plenty this morning before I had to get ready for my afternoon classes, but he remained slightly reserved around me after we aired out all of the dirty laundry.

I suspect I know why, and that just won't do.

Leaning forward, I place my hands on the armrests of his chair and bend in toward him. His eyes immediately fall to my lips as they get closer to his, and I briefly see his eyes go warm before our mouths press together. I kiss him softly at first, but then slide my tongue in against his in a bold display of seduction.

Pulling my mouth away, I take both his hands in mine and pull him up from the chair. He stands hesitantly, his eyes leery and confused. I turn and walk from the office, tugging what I think is a reluctant Beck behind me.

Right-hand turn, and then to the end of the hallway, where I enter our bedroom.

The minute we cross the threshold, I turn and walk into Beck's space. I loop my arms around his neck, one hand to the back of his head, and I pull him back down to me for another kiss. He doesn't hesitate and this emboldens me. I make the kiss deep and wet and I moan my need into his mouth.

But I need more. I step in closer, press my body into his, and feel him growing hard against me. Even as Beck groans from the contact, his hands are at my shoulders pushing me back.

When I open my eyes, he's staring back at me with wariness. "Are you hungry? Want to go out and get some dinner?"

"No," I say as I drop my hand down to his crotch and palm his erection. And thank God he has an erection. I think I would curl into myself and die if he wasn't turned on by me. "I want you to fuck me."

"Sela," Beck says in a patronizing tone that I know he just can't help, and his hand comes to cover mine. "There's no rush—"

"But there is," I say, squeezing him. "We may have all our secrets out on the table, but there's still something standing in our way. We cannot let what JT did to me come between us."

"It won't," he assures me quickly. "But things are raw right now. I want you to be comfortable—"

"Are you grossed out about what he did?" I butt in.

"What?" he exclaims.

"Does it turn you off . . . knowing what he did to me?"

"God no," he practically barks at me with agitation. "But this complicates things a bit. I don't know how you feel and—"

"Don't," I say urgently as I go to my tiptoes. I brush my lips against his softly, and then whisper against his mouth. "Don't treat me like I'm breakable. I couldn't stand it if you did that to me. I need you to show me that you believe I'm strong, and beautiful, and as tough as bricks. If you don't believe that about me, I won't believe it about myself."

I tip my head back, look into his eyes, and plead with him. "I need you to make me feel like I'm normal, Beck."

"Christ," he mutters, and then his hand is grasping the back of my head, fingers fisted tight in my hair. He slams his mouth down on mine while he bends his knees, dips, and with his other arm, hauls me up his body. My legs wrap around his waist and I tilt my face to get a better angle to deepen our kiss.

I roll my tongue against his, my fingers digging down deep into his shoulders. My hips rotate, trying to get contact with his dick and I make an odd keening noise when I can't get some friction going.

Moving a hand from shoulder to the back of his head, I grip his hair hard and tug his head back at the same time I rip my mouth from his. We stare at each other, his eyes blazing with a mixture of lust and tenderness.

"Don't hold back on me, Beck. Please don't hold back."

"Sela," he rasps out as a touch of worry filters into his gaze. "I can't help but treat you as precious. That's not the same as breakable."

"Understood. You can whisper sweet, precious words to me, but you better be fucking me hard while you do it."

"Jesus," he mutters, and his mouth is back on mine again.

He kisses me for all of maybe two, three seconds, then he turns his body toward the bed. Slipping his hands under my armpits, he dislodges my hold on him and throws me onto the mattress.

"Get naked," he commands, and I don't hesitate a single second. My hands work my clothes while Beck does the same, our eyes pinned on each other. I falter only a moment when his pants and underwear come off and his cock angles upward in eager anticipation. And God . . . my mouth waters at the sight.

Then we are naked and he is covering me.

I sigh with blissful abandon as he kisses me again, urgent and desperate movements of his mouth against mine. His hands roam all over me. Gentle fingertips against my collarbone followed by a hard pinch to my nipple. His thumb pressing in slightly and dragging down my ribs, which tickles and turns me on with equal measure. His tongue in my belly button, swirling in a teasing manner, followed by a bite to my hip bone.

Beck moves down my body and I tense up—in a good way, that is—waiting for his mouth to connect to me. For whatever reasons that I've never bothered to ask him, the man loves to work his mouth between my legs. He's so goddamn good at it he can make me come almost instantly.

But right now, he teases all around my money spot with soft kisses and licks to my bare mound. His fingers press all around my pussy but don't slip inside. He tortures me until my hips are thrusting upward in a desperate need for more contact.

And finally . . . finally he gives me what I need. Thumbs peeling me apart and a swirl of his tongue in a figure-eight pattern over my clit.

"Yes," I groan, my back arching up off the bed.

Beck's entire mouth closes over me and he groans in delight when he sticks his tongue inside me as deep as he can get it, lashing it side to side within me. My eyes roll into the back of my head, and I'm on the verge of splintering.

"Sela," Beck says softly, and I lift my head to put hazy eyes on him.

He stares up my body at me intently. "You see this?"

Beck dips his head and strokes his tongue up my center. Pulling it back into his mouth, he licks his lips in an exaggerated fashion.

"This right here," he says, giving me another lick and then staring back up at me. "This is mine. There is nothing down here but you and me. Sela's pussy and my mouth, and that's the only thing here. Doesn't matter what happened in the past. That's done and it's gone. Completely gone. Just your beautiful pussy and my mouth, and well . . . eventually my cock, but that's all there is here. All there ever will be. I don't see anything in front of me other than a stunning woman who's body belongs solely to me, and when I look upon it, I know without a doubt it was created for me. Nothing before me matters, you understand that?"

I blink my eyes hard to fight back the tears that want to well up. His words are coarse and beautiful, sexy and sweet. Only a man such as the one between my legs right now could talk about cock and pussy and make it almost sound like he's saying he loves me. My heart thumps in adoration.

"Tell me you understand so I can make you come and then fuck you hard," he says with a grin.

"I understand," I tell him with a tender smile.

His eyes soften and he mumbles, "My pussy," before he descends back on me again.

My orgasm comes quick and hits me hard, and it's a product more of his words than of his touch, but I revel in it all the same.

"That's it," Beck whispers as he presses kisses on my stomach while he crawls back up my body. He's in control and fluidly raises one of my legs with a hand to the back of my knee, presses his cock right to my entrance, and surges up and into me.

"Ooohhhh," I moan over the thick invasion deep inside of me.

"Christ, that feels good," Beck says with his mouth pressed into my neck.

His hips move, his cock slides back, almost to the tip. Beck lifts his face and stares at me before surging in again. He bottoms out inside me hard and grunts out his pleasure from the feeling.

Back out again, slow . . . measured . . . deliberate.

Eyes connected to me.

Slam.

Back into me again.

His actions are leisurely, his gaze is tender, and his cock is dominating.

It's exactly what I needed to assure me that Beck doesn't see me as a victim. His mouth between my legs and his declaration of possession was what I needed for Beck to assure me I was still as beautiful to him as ever, despite the perverted things done to my body ten years ago.

Beck continues to pull out slowly, ram back into me with bruising reclamation. His pace picks up only slightly, but his fucking of me is deliberately possessive. His actions speak to me loudly, and as he pushes me closer and closer to another orgasm, I feel my heart becoming more and more enslaved to him.

We'll work this out . . . whatever needs to be done about JT.

But that's a side issue right now.

What's more important is what we have between us, and I vow that's where I'm going to put my attention from this moment forward.

. . . .

CHAPTER 10

Beck

I lean my elbow on the kitchen island counter, the fingers on my other hand moving over the track pad on my laptop to pull up my calendar.

"Move Thursday's ideation session to week after next," I tell Linda, who is listening in via my phone lying on the counter in speaker mode. "Cancel tomorrow's meeting with JT and just ask him to email me the proposed business and marketing plans. We don't need a meeting for that."

"Got it," she says over the speaker. "What about the second round reviews of the video component? Programming is slated to begin changes on Monday."

"I'll work on those remotely," I tell her.

Hopefully, remotely means far, far away from here if I can convince Sela to be impulsive with me.

"Anything else?" Her tone is sharp and brisk. She's in full executive secretary mode.

"Yeah," I say as a thought strikes me. "Why don't you take the rest of the week off too."

"Just because you won't be in the office doesn't mean there's not work to do," she chides me.

"Yeah, well, I say you can ignore the work and take the time off," I counter.

"We'll see," is all she says, but I can hear the smile in her voice. "Let me know where you're going and I'll make the reservations for you."

"Thanks, Linda," I say before reaching over to my phone and disconnecting the call.

As I grab my cup of coffee beside my laptop, my eyes land on Sela, who's walking into the main living area. She gives a big yawn and scratches the skin on her belly, which is peeking out beneath the hem of a tight tank she wore to bed.

"Why are you up so early?" she asks, her voice still heavy with sleep.

And let's face it. She didn't get much last night, as we had a few days to make up for in the sex department.

I'm not going to lie . . . that first time was all kinds of awkward at first. Rationally, I knew Sela's rape was years ago, and she had clearly moved past many of her hang-ups. There's no doubt that in our time together, she was giving herself fully to me and enjoyed it as much as I did. Hell, just the way I can make her come so hard and fast was a testament that she was comfortable and trusting with me.

But still . . . scabbed wounds get scraped open and start bleeding, so you handle the body with care. Same goes for emotional wounds, and my instinct was to tread delicately with her.

Sela felt differently though, and I'll admit, her position made sense. She didn't want me stroking her with kid gloves. She wanted to feel alive and normal.

She wanted to feel.

So I felt her up nicely. Fucked her three times last night, feeling her up in between. It reminded me of the night she sucked my dick in the limo, swallowing me down and searching for more. That night we were rabid for one another.

Last night was the same.

I want more of the same today, and the next day, and the day after that.

"Got up around six," I tell her as I push away from the laptop and walk over to the stove. I grab the kettle, turn to the sink, and fill it with enough water to make her a cup of tea. Once it's heating, I turn back toward Sela. She's watching me with a soft smile as she sits on one of the barstools on the opposite side of the island.

While her water heats, I move back to the counter and lean forward on it, the bottoms of my forearms pressed against the cold granite. "Do you have a passport?"

She blinks at me slowly, but nods. "I did a semester in London my junior year of college."

"You did?" I ask, slightly amazed she'd do something so far out of her comfort zone. I've come to find out in just a few short days just how fucked up Sela's existence was for a very long time because of what was done to her. "That was pretty brave."

Sela gives me an impish smile and says, "I did come out of my shell as time went on, you know. I tried new things."

"I'm impressed."

"Yeah, well . . . it's not like I backpacked through the wilds of Kenya or anything," she says in a self-deprecating way, and that causes me to laugh.

"Okay . . . so let's pack up and catch a flight out of here tonight. We can go wherever you want. Paris, Vienna, Berlin, Prague."

"Are you serious?" she asks with her eyebrows practically touching the ceiling.

"Dead fucking serious. We can go for a few weeks, just bum around Europe if you want. Get away from all this craziness and regroup. Or we can go tropical if you want to, because if you only want to wear nothing but a little bikini, I'm down with that too."

"I can't just take off and leave like that."

"You sure as hell can."

"I have school, Beck. Classes I have to attend, work I have to do," she says with an eye roll.

"Drop the classes. Take a semester off," I tell her simply. I mean . . . why the fuck not?

"Just drop my classes? Take a semester off?" Her tone is one of astonishment and exasperation with me.

"Okay, two weeks. I'll pay for it," I say smoothly. "You won't be out any money."

I expect that to piss her off—the not-so-subtle reminder that I paid for her education in return for her giving herself to me—but I'll make her see that I'd buy the world for her right now if I could and wouldn't expect a damn thing in return.

Instead, she narrows her eyes at me. "You are the least impulsive person I know. Beck North doesn't just wake up one morning and decide to jet off to Europe. What's really going on here?"

Taking a deep breath, I push off from the counter and walk around the island until I come up to her stool. She swivels it toward me, her eyes filled with concern.

Blowing out the breath, I take her hands and pull them onto my chest, where I hold them tight. "I need to get away, Sela. I can't go into the office because I can't risk a run-in with JT. I just won't be able to hold it together because all of this is so fresh and raw. I'm afraid of what I might do to him, to our business . . . all of it . . . if I lose control around him. So I want to just leave for a bit, collect ourselves. Take the pack off. Relax and get to know each other better. I don't know what the future has in store, but if JT is going to pay for this, we need to have our ducks in a row. Things are going to get stressful, and I'd like some time with you and away from all of this shit."

Her eyes soften and her head tilts in understanding. "I can't do two weeks. I can only miss three classes in each course."

"A week then," I counteroffer.

"Where would we go?" she asks.

"Wherever you want. I don't care."

"So we'd leave tonight?"

"I'd leave right now if we could, but unfortunately, two things prevent that. First, I have that investigator coming just after lunch. I'm going to hire him to start digging into JT. And second, and probably most important, I need to do laundry, as I'm out of clean underwear."

Sela laughs, and it fills me with hope that we're going to get through this. She leans forward on the stool, presses her bare feet down into the bottom rung, and pushes up to bring her mouth to mine. Just the softest of kisses and an even bigger smile on her face when she pulls back. "Okay. I'm going to go start laundry, then I'm going to message my professors and let them know the classes I'll be missing. You do whatever work you need to get things cleared away."

"So we're going?"

"I'd like to see Vienna," she says as she pushes up from the stool. I step back to give her room and she slides past me, heading over to the kettle, which is now boiling. "Or Prague. That would be nice."

"I'll get Linda to book us flights and make hotel reservations," I say, admiring her ass in some tiny white panties that look virginally sweet.

Then I walk back around the counter to my laptop, and start putting things in order.

• • •

Dennis Flaherty sits across from my desk in my home office, looking nothing like what I thought a sleazy investigator would look like. I was expecting short and portly with perhaps a bad Hawaiian print shirt with mustard stains. He's tall and built solidly, wearing a tailored navy blue suit with a sedate yellow tie. His hair is fiery red but cropped close to his head in a military-style cut. The only other thing I notice is a wedding ring on his left fourth finger.

"You're sizing me up," Dennis says with a smirk.

"That obvious?" I ask him with a laugh.

"I get paid to observe," he says dryly.

"Well, what I'm getting ready to ask you to do might cross some ethical lines. I need some dirty stuff. You look like a financial advisor or banker or something."

Dennis nods in understanding. "Don't let my love of fine Italian silk suits throw you off. I've had plenty of dirt under my nails before."

I glance past Dennis to my open office door. Sela's in our room packing. I asked her if she wanted to sit in on this meeting, but she just shook her head and said, "I'd rather not. I know in painstaking detail what you're going to be talking to him about. I'll let you take this one for the team."

Team.

I liked the sound of that.

"I want you to investigate my partner, Jonathon Townsend. I assume you've done some background research on me?"

"I have. Your partner too. Quite an interesting business you have."

"Well, I want the business for myself and I can't seem to dislodge him. I need something that will convince him to leave."

"How far do you want to go with this?"

"All the way isn't far enough," I tell him smoothly. "I don't care what the cost or what it takes to get me what I need."

"It's personal to you," Dennis observes as he pulls his phone out of the inside breast pocket. I watch as he taps a few times, presumably pulling up an app or something, then his thumbs race across the screen as he types.

"Just making some notes," he says without looking up at me. "I need to know why it's personal so I know which direction you want me looking."

His face tips back up and he pins me with a direct stare. I know he needs to know this, because I want him also looking into fraternity brothers as possible suspects, but it still burns to have someone know what Sela went through. But I have her permission to disclose this sordidness to him, and he came highly recommended, so I press forward.

"Ten years ago, three men raped my girlfriend," I say, and Dennis makes a sound of disgust deep in his throat. "She was drugged and couldn't identify her attackers, but she did remember tiny bits and pieces. One was a distinctive tattoo of a red phoenix on one of her attackers' rib cage."

"She later saw that tattoo and was able to identify him," Dennis surmises, his face now dipped again so he can type into his phone.

"It belongs to my partner, JT . . . otherwise known as Jonathon Townsend," I say, and Dennis' head snaps upward, his eyes wide with surprise.

"You're fucking kidding me?" he practically chokes out.

"I wish I were," I respond grimly. "But it was him, and one of the things I want you to do is look for one of the other suspects that had a matching tattoo on his wrist. It belongs to an inner ring of fraternity brothers."

"I'll need her to give me a drawing or something to go by," Dennis says, still typing.

"No need. I have a matching one on the back of my shoulder."

Again, Dennis' head snaps up, but this time his eyes are angry. "What the fuck is going on here?"

"I was in the same fraternity as JT but three years behind him. Still in prep school when the rape happened, so you can get that look off your face. I'm not sure the tattoo has anything to do with the rape, but clearly at least two of my fraternity brothers were there. I want you to try to identify at least one of the others by the wrist tat. Sela doesn't remember anything other than he was tan and had dark hair."

And that he raped her ass, but I don't tell him that.

"Understood," he says. "What else?"

"I want you to dig deep into JT. Find out what crap he's involved with outside of the business. I know he does drugs and still gets off on spiking women's drinks to rape them, so I'm guessing he's elbow deep in some dirty shit. I want anything I can use to ruin him."

"Why don't you just report the rape to the police?" Dennis asks.

"Sela's considering it, but she's afraid her memory is too spotty for them to investigate him. Also afraid he won't roll on the others. We'd like to see if we can find out the identities of the others first and if there's any other dirt on JT. The police are a last resort."

"When do you want me to start?" he asks, flipping back through his phone . . . presumably for his calendar.

"The minute you walk out that door. And I want you on this exclusively. Turn down your other work or farm it out," I say firmly.

"That'll cost you big," he warns.

I open my middle drawer and pull out my checkbook. It burns like acid deep in my gut knowing that I share DNA with my monster of a half brother, and I'm going to do whatever it takes to make him suffer. It's a good thing I'm fucking rich, and I'd spend every dime I have to help Sela. After pulling a check off, I scratch my signature on the bottom line and hand it to him across the desk. "There's a blank check. Fill in the amount."

My move doesn't seem to surprise Dennis, but he takes the check from me and tucks it into his pocket.

Standing up from his chair, he taps a finger on his phone and says, "Let me get a picture of that tattoo."

Pulling my T-shirt up and over my head, I turn to give my back to Dennis. I hear the sound of his snapping shots before he says, "Got it. Give me two hours to get my desk cleared and I'm all yours until we find what we need."

"Good deal," I tell him with a relieved smile after I tug my shirt back on. I extend a hand to him and he gives it a firm shake.

I've got Dennis digging deep, a week away from the office, and a beautiful girl who wants to hop around Europe with me. For the first time in days, I feel like I can breathe.

. . . .

CHAPTER 11

Sela

I gently tap my spoon against the shell of the soft-boiled egg, which is perched in a white porcelain egg cup. When it was set before me, I didn't have a clue what to do with it. I looked across the table at Beck, who eyed his just as suspiciously. The waitress, however, was not immune to our helpless looks and had clearly encountered her share of ignorant American tourists, and showed Beck how to tap through the top quarter of the shell and twist it off so he could get to the egg inside.

We're sitting at a coveted window table in the Café Schwarzenberg, one of the first true Viennese coffeehouses, which was built in 1861. We missed our connecting flight from Zurich to Vienna, which precipitated a four-hour delay whereby we had to hang out in the airport, only to learn when we arrived at the Grand Hotel Wein early this morning that our room wasn't ready. Apparently some Arab sheik was also staying at the hotel and our room had been mistakenly given to one of his security detail. We were assured they would ready another room for us immediately and suggested we have some breakfast at Café Schwarzenberg, which was just down the block off the Kärntner Ring. I was skeptical about the sheik story, but just as we were making our way out the front double doors, we were astounded to see about twenty reporters spring up from chairs all around the lobby and scurry toward the bank of elevators. Sure enough, a man dressed in full Lawrence of Arabia style stepped out surrounded by five body-guards dressed in black suits, black sunglasses, and wire mics in their ears. They pushed their way through the crowd and Beck took my elbow, pulling me backward to give them passage. The sheik walked right out the door and into an awaiting nondescript black car, with two identical cars behind that carried his bodyguards.

With a sharp whack against my egg, which causes a piece of shell to shoot across the table, I blow off the top of my egg, caus-ing yellow yolk to leak all over the place. I give a disgruntled sigh as Beck laughs at me and push the egg cup away. Instead, I pull a croissant off the side plate and break off a piece.

And oh God . . . I'm not sure anything more delicious has ever been in my mouth. I stifle a moan and put a larger piece be-tween my lips before chewing on it slowly so I can savor.

"What do you think we should do today?" Beck asks as he takes the tiny egg spoon and pulls out some of the white flesh covered in warm yolk from the inside of the shell.

"I'm tired as hell," I say after swallowing, and then punctuate it with a yawn. "But I'm excited to get out and explore. Maybe just walk around the city a bit. Nap in the afternoon so we can get our inner clocks adjusted."

"We should definitely take it easy today," Beck says with a nod, and takes another perfect scoop of egg from his waitress-cracked shell. "You have us booked solid with stuff over the next four days, so this might be our only day to relax."

It's true. I picked up a guidebook about Vienna in the San Francisco airport and I'm trying to pack in as much sightseeing as I can. We're going to tour the Hofburg and Schönbrunn imperial palaces; watch the world-renowned Lipizzan horses perform at the Spanische Hofreitschule Winter Riding School; and take in a performance at the famous Vienna State Opera. We've got the concierge trying to get us tickets to tomorrow night's performance of the Vienna Boys Choir performing at Hofburg Chapel in the Imperial Palace, and I plan to gorge myself on stunning architecture wherever we walk, Wiener schnitzel, and Viennese coffee in between. Because this coffee—I put my croissant down in favor of a sip of the creamy, sweet goodness—is fucking phenomenal. I could totally drink this in place of tea if I could figure out how to make it when we get back home.

"Thank you for doing this," Beck says as he puts his egg spoon down and picks up his coffee. He went with regular black.

I smile at him over the edge of my cup. "Like it was so hard to accept an offer to jet off to Europe with you."

"You had school obligations," he points out.

"Still have them when I go back," I say matter-of-factly. "But you were right . . . you needed a break from the craziness that I laid on your doorstep."

"You needed a break too, Sela. We've got to tread carefully when we go after JT, so we need our wits about us."

"You think Dennis will find something?" I ask before taking another sip. Beck had filled me in on their meeting and right now he was supposedly digging into JT's life.

"I guarantee you there's something," Beck snarls with hatred for his partner. "His soul is black."

"I'm sorry this is hurting you," I say quietly before placing my cup down. "Especially since he's . . . you know . . . your brother and all."

"Hey," Beck says as he puts his own coffee down so his hand can take mine. He squeezes and my eyes lift to his. "He's not my brother. We might share my father's DNA, but he's otherwise dead to me. Don't worry about my feelings on that matter, because the only ones I have now are disgust and hate toward him."

"Still," I say as my head turns to the left and I look out over the sidewalk, which is becoming increasingly busier as the morning wears on. "You probably would have been better off never knowing this. You know . . . the sweetness of ignorance and all that."

"I'd rather have you, even if this shit comes with it," he assures me. "You're more than worth it."

I smile, trying to blink back the stinging in my eyes caused by his words. "By the way, how is it that you're related and you know about it but he doesn't?"

I've been curious about this, as well as other things we haven't been able to discuss. An airplane isn't a very conducive place to talk about such sordid details.

Beck releases my hand and picks his coffee back up. He takes a sip and swallows with a grimace. "My parents and JT's parents have been friends long before any of us kids were ever conceived. When I was about nine, I was playing in my dad's office, under his desk. They had a fancy dinner party going on and I was bored. At any rate, my dad and JT's mom came in and I didn't come out of hiding. Knew my dad would be pissed to find me in there. So I hid under that desk while he fucked her right on the other side, and then later, I listened as they talked about JT."

My hand rises involuntarily to cover my mouth in shock. He was just a kid . . . listening to that. Did he even understand what they were doing?

"What did they say?" I whispered.

"His mom was telling my dad about JT getting in trouble at school. I wasn't half paying attention at first because they'd just had sex five feet from me and I wasn't sure what the fuck that was all about."

I can't help the snort that comes out, but then I clear my throat and look at him with serious eyes.

"At any rate, they started fighting about JT. My dad suggested moving him to another school, and his mom didn't want that, and then Dad got really angry and said, 'Well . . . he's my son, so I should have a say-so.'"

"Oh my God."

"Right? I suddenly started paying attention to what they were saying. They kept arguing about my dad's role in JT's life, and it was clear that JT's dad—the man who raised him, that is—had no clue he wasn't his son. It was clear that no one knew about it except those two."

"So you've held on to this secret since then?" I ask, amazed that someone so young would carry such a terrible weight.

Beck shakes his head. "I told my dad I knew a few years ago. We'd gotten into an argument about Caroline actually. The lengths my family will go to keep their precious secrets. I got pissed and just confronted him about it."

"Did he deny it?"

"No," Beck says with a wry smile. "But he instructed me that I was to forget about it and never mention it again."

I watch as Beck takes another sip of his coffee, fiddles with the end of his croissant. I take a breath and share something that's been on my mind. "Lengths your family would go to keep secrets. An argument about Caroline. You're talking about her rape, right?"

Beck's eyes slide up to mine and they're filled with anger-laced pain. "My parents didn't want Caroline to report her rape to the police. They didn't want the public scrutiny."

"But rape victims' names are held secret," I say in defense of Caroline. I know this from personal experience.

With a grimace, Beck says, "Try telling that to them. They didn't want to take the chance."

"So what happened?"

"I took Caroline to the police station and stood by her while she reported it," he says softly. "My parents never acknowledged it, refused to support her, and as you can imagine, that's what drove Caroline away. She hasn't talked to them since."

"That's awful," I say with disgust. "I'm sorry, but your parents sound like horrible people."

"They are," he agrees with a rueful smile. "They're nothing like your parents. They had your back all the way, didn't they?"

I lower my eyes to my coffee cup and remember fondly their almost-perfect handling of a brutalized daughter. Outrage over what happened to me, validation I did nothing wrong—although I was loath to ever believe that—protectiveness to make me feel safe, and an open, honest environment in which I could process my feelings.

"They were amazing," is all I can say to Beck about them.

"Well, my parents aren't worth a fucking damn and Caroline's glad to be rid of them."

"If you don't mind, could you tell me what happened to Caroline? The experience has also affected you, given you a better understanding of what I went through, but I'd like to know just what happened."

Beck leans forward and puts his elbows on the table. His eyes are clear with honesty but no less clouded with pain. "I don't think she'd mind me telling you. It might be good for you two to talk."

I nod quickly because I'm feeling all kinds of bad that Caroline didn't have the support she needed.

"It happened almost five years ago about this time of year. My parents were having their annual Christmas party, and both of us were attending as dutiful children. Caroline had just turned twenty the month before."

I hold a hand out, do some mental calculation on my fingers, and say, "So Caroline is a year younger than me."

Beck nods. "We left the party after only a few hours, but Caroline was drunk, because that's really the only way to get through being around my parents. This guy she had brought as a date drove her home so I figured she'd be okay, you know?"

His voice has taken on a guilt-filled tone, which causes my hand to fly out to grab his. I squeeze hard . . . painfully hard until his eyes focus on me. "Don't. Don't even go there. You couldn't have known and it could have happened anywhere."

Without acknowledging my words but giving me a return squeeze, which causes my grip to loosen slightly, he continues. "She doesn't really remember much about it. Doesn't remember the drive home, or getting into her apartment. Just that she woke up the next morning, and she . . . well, could tell she'd had rough sex and that protection wasn't used. She had bruises on her throat and wrists; all over her legs and she was bleeding between . . . well, you know."

"God . . . I am so sorry," I whisper.

"She called me right away and I went over to her apartment," Beck says, pulling his hand from mine so he can take another sip of coffee. "Her memory was spotty, she was drunk, and she wasn't sure if it was consensual. She felt—"

"Responsible," I supply automatically.

"Yes . . . blamed herself. But given her condition, I didn't think it was consensual and I asked Caroline point-blank if she was the type to give it up on the first date."

"That was the first time she'd been out with that guy?"

"Michael Schaefer is his name. She'd met him at school. He was the exact opposite of the type of guy my parents would approve of, which is exactly why she brought him."

My memory of seeing the folder in Beck's office as I was

searching it slams into me. It had SCHAEFER INVESTIGATION written on the tab. "He was arrested?"

"She didn't want to report it at first because she couldn't be a hundred percent sure it was rape. She didn't want to ruin him if it was consensual, but I kept after her. She wanted to take a shower, get cleaned up, but I wouldn't let her. It was awful, knowing what happened to her and arguing with her to keep that fucker's semen inside of her so we could go to the police with it."

I can't control the sudden wave of tears that fill my eyes. I know exactly what it feels like to have your rapist's semen on you, and it's the most disgusting thing you could ever imagine. Even now, nausea roils my stomach, threatening to curdle my Viennese coffee.

"What got her to change her mind?" I ask as I blink my eyes hastily.

"I felt the need to get our parents involved, hoping they'd help to encourage her to report it," he says with a disdainful laugh.

And I know what he's going to say, so I say it instead with all the disgust I can muster. "Let me guess . . . they did the opposite. Told her not to report it because it would bring shame on the family. They made her feel fucking shame, didn't they?"

"Yup," Beck says as he points a finger at me and nods. "But it only goes to show you they didn't know their daughter. Caroline took that as a challenge, and it actually strengthened her spirit. She and I always banded together against our parents, so the minute they staked their position in opposition to me, she was spitting nails and eager to report it."

"What happened?"

"They picked up Michael Schaefer and interviewed him. He denied it, stating he dropped her off at her apartment. Didn't walk her to her door . . . just pulled up in front and then took off."

"A real gentleman," I grumble.

"It's why she chose him to go to my parents' party. He was a lowlife. But he wasn't a rapist."

My eyebrows shoot up. I wasn't expecting that. "He wasn't?"

"He volunteered DNA and it excluded him."

"So someone got her at her apartment?"

Beck nods, his lips flat and eyes glinting with menace. "We assume she was ambushed."

"That's horrific. I'm just . . . I don't even know what to say."

He doesn't respond, but picks off a piece of croissant and nibbles on it.

"So that's why Caroline has nothing to do with your parents," I continue. "They didn't believe her; made her feel shameful, and she cut them out."

"It's part of it," Beck says, pulling off another piece of croissant. He waves it at me as he says, "But it more has to do with the fact that once Caroline found out she was pregnant, they wanted her to get an abortion."

At this, my jaw drops open in astonishment. "Ally . . . was conceived by the rape?"

"She was," he says, and his eyes grow soft at just the mention of her. "Caroline refused a morning-after pill at the hospital. She wasn't going to take the chance of killing a life if she was pregnant. My parents went berserk when they found out. Really tried to strong-arm her into aborting her own daughter, but Caroline would never, ever do that. They were wasting their energy and ensuring that Caroline would forever be gone from their life."

"Your parents are absolute shits, Beck. I'm sorry to say that, but they really are."

"Agreed," he says with a wry smile. "And I hope you understand a little why that makes me the way I am. Why I flipped out when I thought you were lying to me. When I found you in my office. I just fucking hate deception and smoke and mirrors. If it's not my father hiding his paternity of JT, it's both my parents shaming Caroline for getting raped and wanting to keep it a secret. It's just . . . I can't fucking stand it."

My eyes slide back out to the street briefly back to him. "I get it. I understand why you did what you did."

"I'm still really sorry for it," he offers.

"Water under the bridge," I smile at him. "So I assume Caroline's rapist was never caught?"

Shaking his head, Beck leans back in his chair. "No. The police checked out surveillance videos in the area, but there wasn't anything that gave a direct line of sight to her apartment. You could see Michael Schaefer dropping her off in the parking lot and then driving off, but no angle provided a clear shot of her apartment door. No witnesses either. DNA didn't match up to any known criminals."

My fingers play with my croissant, but I don't take any more of it. Instead, I put my hands in my lap and lean a little farther over the table. "Beck . . . will you tell Caroline what happened to me? I want her to know she's not alone in what it feels like not to know, and that maybe it's even worse knowing. I want her to be able to talk to me if she wants."

Beck's smile lights his face and he leans forward as well, even farther than I do, raises from his seat, and places his lips gently against mine before saying, "Caroline adores you, and I'm sure she'd be greatly comforted to share in this with you. You are amazing, Sela."

My sigh fans out across his lips before I press in and accept the kiss he had hovering there. When we pull back, I tell him, "Thank you for sharing that with me."

"I'll share everything with you from now on," he assures me. "And you'll do the same with me."

"That I will. Everything."

. . . .

CHAPTER 12

Beck

We're in a private box at the Wiener Staatsoper, otherwise known as the Vienna State Opera. Completed in 1869 under the Hapsburg monarchy, it's built in the neo-Renaissance style—whatever the fuck that means—by Josef Hlavka. He was a world-renowned Czech architect and contractor, and I'm sure I'll forget his name come tomorrow.

But I know it today because since we had tickets to attend the opera *Tosca* at the Vienna State Opera tonight, Sela insisted we do a behind-the-scenes tour of the opera house about five hours ago. I was not overly fond of this idea, because I hate opera, and I was already going to be subjected to it for about three hours tonight. But Sela was so excited, and because I most certainly do not hate Sela, and actually like her more than I've ever liked another woman in my life, I easily gave in to her ludicrous idea.

So in addition to touring Schönbrunn Palace this morning, we spent another two hours walking through this massive structure, being appropriately impressed when our tour guide pointed out the plinths and buttresses made of Wöllersdorfer and Kaisersteinbruch stone, or the hand-carved statues, or even the painted ceilings set amid gilded panels. I grudgingly admit it's an amazingly beautiful building, but I didn't expect to be spending five full hours of my life inside of it.

I suppose the only thing that makes it bearable is that Sela looks amazing tonight. We had not packed anything that would be worthy of an evening in a luxury box at the Staatsoper, but Linda worked magic and found us a boutique that could outfit Sela in a stunning, deep-red gown that sits off her shoulders and dips low into her cleavage. The top of the bodice is fitted, but the skirt portion is long and flowing and swishes beautifully when she walks. I was also able to get a tuxedo at the same boutique, and we were considered presentable as we walked out of the Grand Hotel Wein tonight to get into our hired Mercedes that would take us to the opera.

"Excuse me, Mr. North," I hear from behind me, and I turn in my heavy chair with gold carved accents and plush red velvet cushions to see the private waiter assigned to our box. "Would you care for something to drink?"

So far, we haven't run into much of a language barrier. Schools here require English as a second language, and once you're identified as American, the Austrians are happy to practice their skills. The only issue we had was today at lunch; we chose a restaurant that apparently saw little in the way of tourists, as our waiter couldn't speak a lick of English. She ended up miming the menu to us, and I think I chose the rabbit, but I'm not quite sure.

"Do you want anything Sela?" I ask as I turn to look at her sitting next to me. She's leaning forward in her chair to gaze over the banister at the seats below us.

She tilts her face my way and just shakes her head with a sweet smile. "I'm good."

"Nothing for us right now," I tell the waiter, who nods and starts to back out of our box. "But maybe later."

"Of course," he says. "I'll check back."

Once the door is closed, I lean forward alongside Sela and peer over. We didn't get a chance to see the interior from this perspective today on our tour. With people filing in and the chatter of eager patrons, it doesn't seem as vast and cavernous as it did when we were walking down below.

We're seated in the very middle balcony box on the third tier. As the venue curves in a broad horseshoe around the perimeter, we can't see anything to our immediate left or right, but can vaguely make out the people in the boxes on the ends. I suppose if we had those weird opera glasses, that would help.

"Isn't this place fantastic?" Sela murmurs as she rests her chin on her forearms, which are propped on the banister as she looks out over the crowd. "I'd never have been able to do something like this if I hadn't met you."

She turns her face, chin still resting on her arms, and gives me a smile filled with gratitude and tenderness. It causes my breath to hitch, because it's the most expressive I've ever seen her, and she's more beautiful than I can ever imagine anything being.

Reaching out, I carefully cup my hand behind her neck, very aware not to mess up her long locks curled and pinned on top of her head. I squeeze and lean closer to her. "I'd gladly take the tour of this opera house every day for the rest of my life if it made you happy."

Sela chuckles with amusement and her eyes shine even brighter. "Hated it that much, did you?"

"Not at all," I tell her smoothly. "When I was bored, I just stared at your ass the entire time. So that means I very much enjoyed the tour today."

"Pervert," she says affectionately, and pulls back from the balcony. It causes my hand to fall away from her, but I still take a moment to let my fingers travel over her bare shoulder. It also fills me with no small measure of pride when she shivers from that touch.

The lights start to dim, and from the orchestra pit just in front of the stage, a long low note from a cello sounds. Looks like the show is getting ready to start.

My chair sits beside Sela's so closely it's an easy reach for me to grab her hand and pull it over onto my lap to hold. She gives me an acknowledging squeeze but sits up straighter in her chair, eager for the performance to start.

I lean casually to the right, into her space, and put my lips near her ear. "I think I forgot to tell you . . . but you look stunning tonight."

Without taking her eyes off the stage, she whispers out of the side of her mouth. "You didn't forget. You told me once at the hotel and once in the car on the way here."

"Huh," I whisper back. "Well, I'm telling you again."

"Shhh," she admonishes me as the music starts . . . a slow build of violins, cellos, and flutes. "It's starting."

I don't move back over, but lean just a tad closer until my lips brush her ears. "You know . . . it's so dark in here now, no one could see into this box. We could do all sorts of naughty things in here."

I expect her to chastise me again, maybe even push me away in exasperation so I don't ruin this experience for her. Instead, her head swivels and I can see the flickering of the stage lights in her blue eyes as she stares at me intently.

"You're right," she murmurs, twisting her hand from mine and placing her palm at the top of my thigh. Her fingers press in and she stares at me just a moment longer before turning her gaze back to the stage. "There are indeed all kinds of naughty things we can do in here."

Turns out, the most naughty of things that Sela had envisioned included us fucking in that box. After the second intermission and after she shooed away the waiter who had come to check on us for a third time, and after the lights dimmed once again, Sela made her move.

Tugged me right up from my chair by a sure but delicate grip on my hand, and led me into the shadows of the back corner of the box, right where the door hinges meet the wall. As Cavaradossi sang "E Lucevan le Stelle," I could only truly concentrate on the fact that Sela had dropped to her knees and was licking all around my cock. It wasn't just naughty . . . it was exquisitely sinful that we'd degrade the luxury of the Staatsoper in that way. My ears completely tuned out Puccini when Sela somehow managed to climb my body and sank her gloriously wet, tight pussy onto me. I merely made a quarter turn, which placed her back against the wall, put my hands under her ass, and proceeded to fuck her as hard as I could. Thank God the music was bold and the venue perfectly arranged so it infiltrated every nook and cranny of the place, because at one point Sela shouted out as she started to come. I had to slap a hand quickly over her mouth, but I was so goddamned turned on it wasn't long before I was groaning loudly with my face pressed into her throat as I unloaded within her.

Now that is the type of opera I could get behind seeing more often.

We had a nightcap in the hotel lobby after we returned, and while I couldn't imagine a night passing when I wouldn't be sunk deep inside of Sela's body, we actually both fell asleep almost immediately when we crawled under the covers. Not sure if it was the nonstop sightseeing we've done the last four days, the amazing food, or maybe just the adrenaline high of the fantastic fucking we did at the opera, but we both conked out quickly.

I know I slept deeply because I was fairly groggy when I woke up at almost four A.M. needing to take a piss. I did my business, washed my hands, and swished some mouthwash around my tongue and teeth, then gargling before spitting it out. I was tired and could easily fall back asleep, but I also felt awake enough that I could spend some quality time with Sela's body. We're on vacation; tomorrow is our last day before we leave for the States, and if I wake Sela and keep us both up for a few hours, there's nothing preventing us from going right back to sleep after.

Before heading back to bed, I grab my phone charging on the desk in our suite and quickly check my messages. JT has been texting me almost every day, demanding I respond to him.

The first one came the evening we left for Vienna. *"Dude . . . Linda said you're going to Vienna? That's a surprise. What's up with that?"*

I ignored it, afraid my response would be something along the lines of, *"I know what you did you low-life piece of shit and I'm going to make it my mission to ruin you."*

He sent follow-up texts periodically over the next four days that got increasingly more angry.

"Hope your vacation is going well. Call me. Need to discuss some business.

Beck . . . I need to talk to you. I've got to give a thumbs-up or thumbs-down on the Nicholson-Meyers project. Call me.

Will you fucking call me? I need to talk to you asap.

I don't know what the fuck is going on, but I've about had it. Call me."

I ignored every single one of these, as well as the few times he actually tried to call me. I merely instructed Linda to pass along to JT that I was in full-vacation mode and was not accepting any business calls or texts until I returned stateside. That must have done the trick, because it's going on almost forty-eight hours and I haven't heard anything from him.

I'm absolutely dreading my first day back in the office and I haven't a clue as to how to handle him. At this point, I'm thinking of working from home indefinitely to avoid him until I can figure a way to bring him down.

Tapping on my email icon, I scroll through the messages. All those from Linda I'll read tomorrow. One from JT looks like he just forwarded an article from *Investor's Weekly*, and although it probably has some helpful information, I delete the fucking thing so I don't have to even look at JT's name.

Sliding my finger down the screen, I stop on an email from Dennis Flaherty sent a little over an hour ago.

The subject line is simple and causes my heart to race: *I Hit Pay Dirt*.

The messages only has two words: *Call me*.

I shoot a quick glance at Sela, and assured that she's sleeping soundly, I walk into the bathroom and shut the door behind me. It's only seven P.M. back in the States, and the worst I'd be doing is interrupting his dinner, so I don't hesitate in dialing his number.

He answers on the second ring by saying, "Figured I'd be hearing from you fairly soon, although it's what . . . four A.M. there? You're up awful early."

I don't bother to engage the polite small talk. "What did you find?"

Dennis is all business and gets to the heart of the matter. "Turns out drugs and abusing women isn't your partner's only addictions. Appears he's got a bit of a gambling problem."

This does not surprise me, but I also don't know if this can help me. "How big of a problem?"

"He is in deep, and I mean way deep to some nasty people here in San Francisco who are backed by even nastier people in Vegas."

"But he doesn't go to Vegas," I say dumbly. At least I don't think he does. Not that I'm really privy to JT's plans, but I don't ever recall him taking any trips to Vegas.

"You don't have to go to Vegas to enjoy their high-dollar stakes."

"What does he bet on?" I ask curiously.

"The question should be 'what doesn't he bet on?' He's into everything. High-dollar online poker, horses, boxing, UFC fights, Rose Bowl winner, Super Bowl winner, the sex of Princess Kate and Prince William's next child. Whatever the fuck you can bet on, JT's laying down money on it."

"So how is this pay dirt?" I ask hesitantly.

"Because he is leveraged to the hilt. He's got almost two million dollars out on unpaid bets he owes and Vegas wants to collect."

"I don't understand," I say stupidly. "JT's not poor. Two million isn't anything to sneeze at, but he should easily be able to come up with that."

Dennis chuckles into the phone and I can hear the flat-out amusement within the guttural sound. "JT *is* poor Beck. He's got maybe a couple hundred grand in liquid assets, but everything else is either gone or tied up. Hell, he could legitimately file for bankruptcy."

"Gone?" I'm just not putting this together. It's not adding up.

"How in the hell do you think a man who lives his lifestyle could afford a two-million-dollar mark owing to a bookie? You can't wear a new three-thousand-dollar suit every day of the week, drive a five-hundred-thousand-dollar sports car, and have a spare three-hundred-thousand-dollar sports car sitting in your garage. You can't buy toy submarines and take five-figure vacations several times a year. He hemorrhages money faster than it's replenished. You and Mr. Townsend take only a modest salary from The Sugar Bowl in comparison to the revenues, am I right?"

He's right about that. "Yeah . . . we each get roughly five hundred thousand per year. The rest is all in stock options, long-term, high-yield investments."

"Stuff that can't be touched," Dennis adds.

"But he had trust monies he put into The Sugar Bowl when we first started it. Our profits first year paid those back to him. He should be flush with at least a couple million."

"That wasn't his money he put in," Dennis says, almost with a cackle of glee to reveal that to me.

"Say what?" I ask, my jaw now hanging open.

"JT's trust was nominal. He had maybe a million in it. His start-up capital into the business was from a loan. And he paid that back to the lender with interest that first year."

"Who was the lender?" I ask, almost believing I have it figured out, but I want to hear it all the same.

Dennis hesitates only a moment, but there's no fear in his voice when he lays it on me. "Your dad . . . Beckett W. North, Sr. made the loan."

This surprises me. Doesn't piss me off, because my dad is an investment banker, and that's what he does. It's just . . . I never thought JT would go to my dad for something like that. Sure, we grew up together and our families did a lot of stuff together, but despite the fact they shared DNA, they just weren't that close, to be honest. I figured JT had to have some brass balls to approach my dad, as it was a risky venture.

Unless . . . JT does know he's really a North and not a

Townsend. That would explain him going to my father for such a large amount of money.

Shaking my head, I put that aside. Doesn't really matter to me how he got that money to start The Sugar Bowl, what matters is the fact he's nearly broke right now.

"This is all fascinating," I tell Dennis. "But how does this help me get him out of my company? It seems to me he'd hold on tighter than ever for the security."

"Listen," Dennis says, his voice dropping an octave lower. "JT could probably scrape up the two million he owes the bookies. He'd take some penalty and tax hits on some of the investments, but he could probably do it. The current predicament he's in isn't going to help you."

"But I sense you know something else that can help me?" I prod.

"There's a UFC fight at Caesar's Palace in three weeks—"

"Mariota versus VanZant," I say automatically, because it's a highly publicized matchup and I've heard plenty about it. Mariota is the reigning welterweight champion. He's undefeated in twelve matches and they say unstoppable. But VanZant wants a shot at him and has dropped almost twenty pounds to move down from light heavyweight to Mariota's weight class. VanZant is a serious underdog, but there are plenty who think he's the one. He's relatively new to the circuit, but the fact he made such a huge weight class move has Vegas all abuzz. Odds are still in favor of Mariota though.

"Apparently, JT is making a last-ditch effort to save his own ass," Dennis explains. "He's gone in double or nothing on his debt to his bookie and laid it all on VanZant to win. If he does, his two million gets paid and he walks away with an equal amount."

"And if he loses?" I ask, but I already sort of know the answer.

"He's probably going to get the shit beat of out him. I'm thinking busted kneecaps at the least, but they might carve out a spleen or something."

Nice. I could totally be down with that.

"But, more than anything, if he loses, he's going to be scrambling for the money. And who do you think he's going to go to to avoid ending up in the hospital?"

"Me," I say firmly. He'll absolutely come to me, and I now see where Dennis is going with this. "I give him the money in exchange for ownership of The Sugar Bowl."

"Exactly," Dennis says with satisfaction.

"How do we ensure JT loses?" I ask, because that's the part that's risky.

"Well," Dennis says hesitantly. "That's going to cost you some money too, but I've got an idea. When are you due back?"

CHAPTER 13

. . . .

Sela

Dennis Flaherty is an interesting character. He's imposingly big, yet looks elegant in a light gray tailored suit with a pale blue hankie in the pocket. His face is boyish with Irish freckled skin, bright red hair, and crystal blue eyes, yet there's a wisdom there that tells me he's seen stuff in his life. Although Beck said he came highly recommended by a friend of his, I can also tell by just looking at him that he's trustworthy. It's a gut instinct, and I'm anxious to hear more of what he has to say about JT.

We flew into San Francisco last night via another layover in Zurich—this time easily making our connecting flight—but Beck and I are feeling the keen effects of jet lag as we all take seats in our living room. With his hand holding mine on the couch, we both watch as Dennis sits in one of the matching white suede armchairs and crosses one leg over the other in sophisticated fashion.

"Where do you want me to start?" Dennis asks as he reaches down beside the chair to a briefcase he deposited there a moment ago, pulling a manila folder from a side pocket. "The info I have on JT or the photos?"

Beck turns to look at me, his eyebrows raised in question for me to make the call.

"The photos," I say with a hard swallow. That will be the hardest part, as evidenced by the thumping of my pulse.

Dennis stands from his chair and walks over to the coffee table. He opens the folder and pulls out a thick stack of photos and lays them out on the coffee table before me. "There are a lot to go through. I narrowed them down as best I could by the descriptions you gave me, the time period, and what Beck could recall of those fraternity brothers who were close friends with JT."

I nod as my eyes start scanning the photos before me. They're all in black and white on glossy paper, with four pictures per page. Leaning forward on the couch, I hover over them while Beck's hand goes to my lower back, where it presses in softly for support.

My eyes scan left to right, first the top row, then the bottom. I flip through page after page of photos, noting dark hair, pale hair, light eyes, dark eyes. They all look nondescript to me and not one of the photos causes an internal reaction.

Shaking my head, I mutter, "I don't know . . . no one looks familiar."

"It's okay," Beck says softly, his hand rubbing in circles against my back. "Take another look."

I do as he asks, flipping back through, a bit slower this time. All the men look back at me with innocent eyes.

"Nothing," I say in frustration, pushing them across the table back at Dennis.

"Doesn't mean he's not in there," Dennis says as he picks up the stack and straightens it before putting the photos back into the folder.

As he turns to sit in the armchair again, I look at Beck. "When I first saw JT on TV, there was a vague recognition. I wasn't sure how I knew him, but there was a familiarity. I don't know that the other men are in that stack Dennis has."

Beck pulls me back onto the couch, wrapping his arms around me. Placing a kiss to my temple, he whispers, "Don't worry. We'll broaden the search. We can head over to Stanford one day and look through all the yearbooks. It will be tedious, but maybe you'll recognize someone that way."

I nod, smiling uncertainly at him before turning my gaze to Dennis. His eyes are kind as he watches me.

"Putting my other attackers aside, how do we handle JT?" I ask him.

"Well," Dennis says with a glint in his eye. "We could force JT to confess his accomplices. The information could be tortured out of him. Probably a personal confession too."

A zing of pure pleasure courses through me and I sit up straighter over Dennis' words. They resonate with my own blood-lust that I've been trying hard to keep at bay.

"That's not a good option at this point," Beck says, and I instantly deflate.

But he's right. We spent a great deal of time talking about this while in Vienna. Although I still sometimes dream of JT's death by my hand, I know deep in my gut I can't do that. Not because I don't think it's justified, but because it's not what's best for me and Beck as a couple. One thing I've managed to understand with great clarity is that Beck has now become the most important thing to me. While I still need to seek justice for myself, I need to balance it with keeping myself safe and ensuring that Beck comes out of this with no damage. Ideally, that means having The Sugar Bowl intact and untainted before JT is made to pay for what he did to me. In this respect, Beck and I have formed a partnership, so to speak, whereby we both can achieve our goals.

"I've decided to go to the police," I tell Dennis as my hand goes to Beck's knee where I squeeze it reassuringly. This was also something we talked about in Vienna, but was a decision that I came to on my own.

"After we get JT out of The Sugar Bowl," Beck amends quickly.

Dennis nods in understanding, but points out the problems with this plan. "Your memory of the tattoo may not be enough to force the district attorney to compel a DNA sample."

"It's a risk," Beck agrees. "But we also have Melissa Fraye. He tried to drug her. Hopefully that will be enough for the DA to investigate JT."

"And he may not turn on his accomplices," Dennis says, but this is also something we considered.

This was the part I was willing to sacrifice if need be. It was what I was willing to give up in order to make sure our two main objectives were reached. JT paid for what he did to me and Beck gets The Sugar Bowl free and clear.

"It's not important," I tell Dennis brusquely.

"It *is* important," Beck says as he turns to face me on the couch. He holds my eyes so he knows that this is troubling to him, but this I already know. We talked this issue to death while sitting on the bank of the Danube River a few days ago, trying to figure out how we could have it all.

I quickly decided that while Dennis has the best idea—beat the shit out of JT until he confesses everything—that is a crime we can't afford to risk. Anything we got out of that wouldn't be admissible.

No. Our best bet was to use my memory of the tattoo to iden-tify my attacker, and leave it up to Lady Justice to force JT to give a DNA sample that would most definitely match the semen taken from my hair that night.

Taking Beck's hand, I squeeze it and say, "Identifying the other men will be the icing on our cake if we can do that, but let's keep our eyes on the prize, okay?"

"So brave," Beck murmurs before giving me a sad smile. He then turns to Dennis and says, "We have our agenda. First is to get JT disconnected from me. That means out of The Sugar Bowl."

"And he needs to be ruined," I add. Dennis' eyes swing from Beck to me with a glow of appreciation, and in that moment, I understand that he's a man who personally understands retribution. I'm dying to know his backstory, but it would be totally in poor taste to ask, I think.

Leaning back in his chair, Dennis folds his hands over his stomach and turns to Beck. "Bottom line . . . JT is cash poor. Since The Sugar Bowl started three years ago and he paid your father back the start-up capital, his living expenses have exceeded his income. That means not only has he squandered every bit of his yearly income on a lavish lifestyle, gambling, and drugs, he's got no appreciable liquid assets he can use to bail himself out. There are some modest investments in mutual funds, but most of his money is tied up in his Sausalito home with little to no equity. His credit cards are maxed out. Again, he might be able to scrape a few million together, but he'd need some time to do it. Rather than try to pay off his debt, he's making the idiotic—and for us, very opportune—decision to double down to his bookie. If he loses, they will want immediate payment. And trust me when I say they will make him hurt to get the money. He'll be desperate for help."

Beck had told me about JT betting double or nothing on the Mariota-VanZant fight that's going to be held on January 2nd. I don't know anything about this sort of stuff, but I didn't have a hard time figuring out that if JT loses, he'll owe four million dollars, and based on what Dennis is saying, he will not be able to come up with that sum.

"How do you know all this stuff?" I ask Dennis with a mixture of amazement and skepticism. "I mean . . . JT's personal finances, his gambling. I mean, how do you even know what he owes to a bookie and what he's betting?"

Gone is the charming look of an Irish boy in an expensive suit and his eyes chill somewhat. It's not enough to scare me, but enough to know that Dennis Flaherty is someone who walks a narrow line, not afraid to step off onto the dark side.

"Plausible deniability" he says coolly, but then tempers the rebuke with somewhat of an understanding smile. "You're safer and more shielded the less you know about my methods. Just know that my resources are not only accurate but infinite, and when the money is right, such as what your boyfriend is shelling out, there isn't much I can't accomplish."

My head swivels to Beck. "Just how much money are you shelling out?"

"No clue," Beck says with a sheepish smile. "I gave him a blank check."

"What the hell, Beck?" I say in exasperation. "You can't just go handing someone a blank check without knowing what exactly you're getting."

"He's getting a way to ruin JT," Dennis says calmly, and my gaze slides back over to him. Gone is the ice in his eyes and instead he holds an amused smile. "But I haven't filled the check out yet, because that all depends on what you want to do from here on out with the information I just gave you."

"So tell me exactly what it will cost," Beck says, his tone now all businesslike as he sits forward on the couch and rests his elbows on his knees.

"How much do you know about the UFC?" he asks, to both of us I believe as his gaze travels back and forth between us.

"A little," Beck says.

"Nothing," I say at the same time.

Dennis leans forward in the chair, matching Beck's posture of elbows resting casually on his knees. "UFC stands for Ultimate Fighting Championship. It's a promotion organization that sponsors bouts between fighters who practice mixed martial arts. MMA has come a long way since its inception in the early nineties when it was a rarely watched sport of just two men in a cage brawling it out with very few rules by which to abide. Today it generates over five hundred million dollars a year in revenue, and its pay-per-view events are becoming as popular as some premium boxing matches."

"That makes it a popular sport to bet on," Beck surmises.

"Exactly," Dennis says with a nod. "But here's why this is an opportunity for you. Most UFC fighters don't make a lot of money. The median pay for a fighter hovers around the twenty-thousand-dollar mark with some bonuses thrown on top for a win."

"Not a lot of money to get your ass kicked," I mutter.

"It's not," Dennis agrees. "Sure, some of the top-billed fighters can earn hundreds of thousands for a match, but those are probably only the top one percent."

"Where does VanZant fall?" Beck asks.

Dennis smiles, because Beck has caught on. "He's undefeated, so he commands a bit more, but he's only getting a hundred thousand for the fight, with a fifty-thousand bonus for the win."

"So he can be bought?" I ask with skepticism.

"Maybe," Dennis says as he pins me with a direct stare. "He'd have to weigh the risk. He could lose to Mariota, who is also undefeated and the reigning champion of his weight class. That would probably cause his earning potential to be crippled. The other risk is of serious injury. Fighters don't last long in this sport, as the risk of debilitating injury is high."

"What are the pros?"

"If he wins, he's looking at potential lucrative endorsements. A higher salary for his next fights, probably with a cut of pay-per-view earnings. A win against Mariota could potentially send him up the ladder with the big boys who can earn half a million to a million on a fight."

"So we have to make an offer to him that can't be refused," Beck says thoughtfully.

"Five hundred thousand," Dennis says matter-of-factly. "Maybe less, but if you want a done deal and you want him to fall believably, I think that's the amount that would do the trick."

"And what?" I say, still unsure about how Dennis could even accomplish something like this. "You're just going to approach him with an offer?"

"Not me," Dennis says vaguely. "But I have a contact who will for a small middleman fee."

"And just how much then would you be filling in that blank check Beck gave you?" I ask.

"For my investigation into JT and his accomplices, the middleman fee to float the offer to VanZant, and VanZant's bribe . . . with Beck's permission I'll fill it in for $675,000. I dispense all the money so the only paper trail is of you paying an investigative service. We can say it's a multiyear retainer for me to contract privately for The Sugar Bowl to vet the Sugar Daddies and Babies."

"No," I say, turning to face Beck on the couch. His head swivels to look at me with raised eyebrows. "It's just too much money. Too much risk."

"Sela," Beck says soothingly as he turns all the way to me and puts one hand on my knee. "Unlike JT, I have not squandered my money and I have plenty of it. That's nothing in the grand scheme of things."

"It's too risky," I maintain, suddenly not feeling good about this. "I mean, even if VanZant loses, you're still banking on JT coming to you for the money. And if you're lucky enough to have him do that, I'm not about to have you hand over four million to satisfy his debt. I can't stomach the thought of you giving JT that type of money."

"It's the only way to get him out of The Sugar Bowl," Beck says softly. "It would be a nominal amount to get sole ownership of The Sugar Bowl, which will earn millions and millions over my lifetime. It's nothing more than a buyout, which is what I'd have to do if he willingly sold to me, and if he willingly sold to me, he'd demand much more than four million dollars. Trust me on that."

I open my mouth to argue, but Dennis cuts me off. "You could come out cheaper."

Both our heads turn his way.

"How's that?" Beck asks.

"Buy his current debt from the bookie," Dennis says simply.

"That wouldn't work," Beck says adamantly. "I'd have no leverage to make him pay. I'm assuming, at the least, his bookie has an enforcer that would impress upon JT the importance of satisfying the debt."

"I'm not finished," Dennis says with a calculated smirk. "Normally you'd buy the debt at a reduced price, which is attractive to the lender because it's guaranteed. But instead, offer to buy it at full price and have the bookie still run a sham double-or-nothing bet. VanZant takes the fall, and the bookie is owed a sham four million. You wouldn't have to pay a damn penny more to him on

JT's behalf when he comes asking for the money, but JT doesn't need to know that. You'd essentially be buying the enforcement."

"That's too complicated," I say, nibbling on a fingernail in worry. Everything we're talking about is illegal as hell, and I have to wonder why I'm suddenly growing a conscience when murder had been my primary agenda in the not-so-distant past.

"Or," Dennis says with an evil glint in his eye. "Let JT make the bet, let him lose, and you promise to pay the bookie. Get it in writing he transfers Sugar Bowl ownership to you, then fuck him over and don't pay a damn dime. Let him take the beating he deserves, then go to the police."

"Fuck JT over?" Beck asks in amazement, and I can tell by the tone of his voice that this appeals greatly to Beck's sense of justice.

"It's still too risky," I say, again trying to be the voice of reason between these two men who are now scenting blood in the water. "We don't even know VanZant will take the fall. Or that JT will come to you for the money. It's a whole bunch of luck you're relying on."

Beck turns my way once again and smirks. "Seems to me I remember a woman who was banking on a whole lot of luck that first night when you planned to confront JT at that mixer."

"Well, I hadn't thought things through—"

"Sela," Beck cuts me off. "These are all good options, and yes . . . luck will be involved. What's the worst that will happen? I won't get JT out of the business cleanly, but we'll still have the option of going to the police."

I stare at Beck, searching deeply into his eyes, hoping to find some measure of comfort over what we're attempting to do. I'm terrified Beck will get so caught up in this he'll fail to look out for his own safety and well-being, but he looks back at me with confidence and surety.

He's asking me to trust him on this and let him help me.

While so much of this still feels wrong, it's the way Beck is looking at me right now that causes me to nod my head in acquiescence.

Beck turns to Dennis. "Make the offer to VanZant. If he bites, we roll forward as planned. Operation Fuck Over JT is now in progress."

"Do you want me to float an offer to buy the debt from his bookie?" Dennis asks.

Beck immediately shakes his head. "No. Like Sela said, that's just too complicated, so let's keep this very simple. Make the offer to VanZant to take the fall. If he does, JT loses the bet and the bookie comes to collect. I'm prepared to pay four million to JT to get him out of The Sugar Bowl. It's a cheap price for the buyout of a business that will generate more than a hundred times that amount over my life."

He then turns his gaze to me and gives me a reassuring smile. I try to levy one back at him, but it's a pale attempt.

Reaching his hand out, he places his palm to my cheek. "Trust me . . . this will work."

"I trust you," I tell him, my smile getting a bit stronger.

Because I do.

Trust this man.

More than anyone else in my life, and I have to believe that we'll both come out of this on top and I'll be vindicated.

. . . .

CHAPTER 14

Beck

Sela was a nervous wreck this morning as she kissed me before I left to come into work today. After Dennis left us Friday afternoon, we had a low-key weekend, preferring to hang at the condo and decorate for Christmas. We were both somehow able to put all the craziness of our plot against JT aside, and instead concentrate on invoking some holiday spirit.

This will be my first Christmas with a girlfriend.

It's Sela's first with a boyfriend.

Two souls who have preferred to be alone for holidays past, now bonded through circumstance, passion, and a focused need for revenge. I'm not sure if that's the stuff that love is built upon, but I know that watching Sela set out her mom's nutcrackers with a fond smile on her face, or helping her cut out sugar cookies that we later burned and still ate anyway, filled me with a satisfaction and warm happiness I've never felt before.

For the entire weekend we transformed the condo into a Christmas wonderland, ate takeout and burned cookies, and fucked—or maybe we made love, I'm not sure—like two people starving for a connection.

We didn't discuss JT or our plan to bring him down once.

Until this Monday morning after I showered and dressed, drank my cup of coffee, and Sela walked with me to the condo door to kiss me goodbye.

"Why the worried look?" I asked her after our lips parted.

"You're going to be seeing JT for the first time since you found out what happened to me," she said with a furrowed brow. "I'm nervous."

"Don't worry," I told her with a confident smile. "I can keep it together."

She knew what I meant by that. Our best chances of getting JT out of The Sugar Bowl all hinged on him coming to me for bailout money. For him to do that, he has to have trust in me. For him to have trust in me, I cannot appear to be anything to him other than a devoted friend and concerned business partner.

In other words, I'm going to have to not only act as if I don't hate the son of a bitch, I'm going to have to pour on a little extra charm to keep him tied to me emotionally over the next two weeks until the fight.

It will require a great deal of acting and a hell of a lot of luck so I don't lose my temper around him. But I'm not worried the way Sela was this morning. I have a driving motivation to make sure this all works. I can see the finish line and Sela is waiting there for me, and nothing is going to stand in my way to get there. If that means I have to sleep with the enemy so to speak for a few weeks, it's a sacrifice I'll gladly make to get what we deserve, and give JT what he most assuredly deserves.

As I pull open the glass front door to the Townsend-North lobby, I take stock of the fact my heartbeat is steady and my palms are cool and dry. Not an ounce of nervousness or worry on my part, and that's because my motivation and need to make this work outweighs any need to let my temper get out of control around JT.

In fact, I'm almost looking forward to seeing the fuckwad. I'll be setting out the bait that will help compel him to come to me when he gets in trouble, and that thought makes me giddy with excitement. Hell . . . I can practically taste the justice on my tongue as I smile at the receptionist when I walk by.

Linda welcomes me back with a wide grin as I approach her desk. "I trust Vienna was to your liking?"

"It was fabulous," I tell her as she hands me a stack of message slips. "You totally are getting a bonus for scoring those tickets to the Vienna State Opera."

"I bet the performance was marvelous," she says wistfully, but I just smile silently on the inside because I was actually thinking about the amazing sex I had with Sela in the private box.

"Is JT in yet?" I ask as I flip through the messages.

"He is," she says as I look back to her. "And he asked that you go see him as soon as you got in. I think you made him anxious with your spontaneous trip away with your girlfriend."

Laughing as I turn toward JT's office, I tell her, "I'll smooth out his ruffled feathers, no worries."

Smooth them out, ease his worries, invite him further into my web.

"Good morning, Mr. North," Karla says in a flat voice as she sees me approaching. His secretary doesn't like me very much, and I'm guessing it's because Linda gets more perks than she does. I reward those who do great work, and sometimes it causes some animosity toward me and my own. Why she just doesn't hate JT because of her poor work environment is beyond me, but apparently it's all my fault he's a douche.

"Good morning, Karla," I say jovially, leveling her my most charming grin. It bounces right off her face set in stone and falls flat between us. "Is JT with anyone?"

"No, sir, but he does have a meeting in fifteen minutes."

"I won't keep him long," I say as I turn toward JT's closed office door. I give two sharp raps with my knuckles and then turn the knob before he even can respond.

JT sits behind his desk, leaning back casually in his office chair. He has one leg propped over the other and is perusing a document in his hand. His face lifts slightly to look at me and then drops back down to the papers in his hand.

"Glad you could come in to work," he says dryly, with an unmistakable hint of censure.

I flop down in the seat opposite him and kick my feet up onto his desk. "Well, hello, JT. It's nice to see you too."

He snorts but keeps reading his document. I take the moment to study him carefully and unobtrusively. JT had been my longstanding friend, and even though I often wanted to throttle him, deep down I always loved him. But now he's an evil monster in my eyes. I find it utterly fascinating that I'm sitting here looking at him with detachment, apparently fully capable of keeping my rage toward him compartmentalized. I think that I have such a sense of moral high ground cushioning me right now, sprinkled with a bit of vigilante justice, that I'm able to view him as a mouse in my game.

I'm the cat, by the way.

"Come on, man," I say with amused affection that tastes slightly bitter on my tongue. "You're not mad I took a week off from work with a gorgeous woman, are you?"

JT doesn't look up at me, but I see the corner of his mouth tip up. "No," he drawls. "I'm mad you wouldn't answer any of my fucking calls or emails."

"Seriously dude . . . have you seen Sela?" I ask with a laugh that I'm pleased sounds genuine. "I was a little preoccupied."

He doesn't respond or look up at me, and I find the sullen silence to suit the egotistical child-man I know him to be.

"JT," I say softly, and because he can hear the seriousness in my voice, he raises his gaze to mine. "I think I love her, man."

With raised eyebrows and mouth slightly agape, he repeats, "You love her?"

Yes, JT. I think I've fallen in love with the woman you raped ten years ago. What I really want to do is kill you. Choke you with my bare hands while you plead with your eyes for me to stop. I want to watch you take your last breath, and then I want to go tell Sela that she's been avenged.

But I can't say that, so I simply say, "I think I do. I mean . . . I can't seem to get enough of her. I've asked her to move in permanently with me, and I think she's the one. You know how you just kind of know?"

JT shakes his head and I'm not surprised when he says, "No. I don't know. Never felt that before for a woman."

Because you're incapable of love you selfish, narcissistic, sociopathic prick.

"I wish you could feel it, buddy," I tell him with a wistful smile. "It's amazing. Finding someone you want to devote your life to."

JT just blinks at me, clearly perplexed. He can't comprehend that level of care.

"Finding a woman who completes you," I continue as I pin him with a fervent look. "A woman that you would do anything for. Defend to the end. Be her knight in shining armor. Make all her worries and hurts go away, no matter the cost."

I'm going to make you pay for what you did to her, you fucking bastard.

"Yeah," I say with a smile leveled at my half brother. "I think I love her."

Tilting his head to the side, he gives me a pointed look. "You've only known her a few weeks."

"Almost a month and a half."

"Still not very long to fall in love," he says skeptically. "Especially for a confirmed bachelor."

Now, let me throw a little more bait out there for you. Make you think you're my guy. Buds to the end. "You think I'm rushing it?"

JT chomps down hard on the bait and sits up straighter in his chair as he tosses down the document. He leans forward, resting his forearms on the desk, and clasps his hands, leveling a serious look at me. "Listen . . . I don't know Sela very well, but dude . . . she's a Sugar Baby. Sugar Babies are all about the money. Now, I'm not saying that's what she's doing, but just remember what her initial agenda was when you first met her."

I have to practically bite down on the inside of my cheek not to laugh out loud, because it's fucking funny that JT would even try to hazard a guess as to what Sela's original agenda was when I first met her. He'd be shocked as shit to know it wasn't to get my money but to murder him in cold blood.

Still, this opportunity is too good to pass up, so I play along with JT's overly concerned, best-friend act. "You think she could be after me for my money?"

JT shrugs, acting nonchalant, but he can't hide the barest hint of malice in his eyes. It sparkles at me, and in this moment, I know for a fact that JT doesn't like Sela. I think about what she told me—about the way he treated her on the way to dinner that night—and it hits me with absolute certainty that JT might even be slightly jealous of her. That she has my attention, and it's becoming more important than my friend and business partner.

"I don't know, buddy," he says somberly. "I just want you to be careful and remember the reason she's a Sugar Baby. It's always about money with them."

Not with Sela, I want to automatically say, because that's the truth. While I know she was grateful for the payment of her student debt, she absolutely shuns my money in all other respects. But JT doesn't need to know how much I've come to respect her. I need him to see us as buddies, cohorts . . . partners to the end.

Until I end him, that is.

I nod along, trying to look grateful for his sage advice. "It makes sense," I say, scratching at my chin. "I mean . . . she doesn't seem to care about my money, but still . . . you're right. I haven't known her that long, and while I'm not ready to give her up fully, maybe I need to put the brakes on . . . slow things down a little."

There's a tint of satisfaction in his eyes, then he gives me a full, dazzling smile. "I've got your back, man. Always."

"Just as I have yours," I tell him with as much fake gratitude and emotion as I can muster.

He holds my gaze, beaming warmth and camaraderie. It makes me slightly nauseated, but I beam my own smile back at him.

"Big plans for Christmas?" JT asks as I stand up from my chair, indicating that our bro chat is over. He stands as well. "I assume you'll make your required appearance at your parents' party this Thursday."

I grimace, and there's no hiding that emotion, but it's okay, because JT knows how I feel about my parents. He knows I generally shun their zest for fame and fortune, which includes the annual Christmas Eve party where they can show off their perfect house and perfect family—minus Caroline and Ally, of course.

"Yeah, I'll be there," I say in a low voice as I turn toward his office door. "You?"

"You know I will be. Not about to pass up that amazing food and liquor," he says with a laugh as he walks out from behind his desk and follows me to the door.

"Will you be bringing Sela?" JT asks, trying to sound casual.

"Because if not, we could go out after the party. Paint the town red or something."

Yeah, fucker. That won't ever happen.

"I'd love to, man," I say sincerely as I open the door before turning slightly to look at him. "But I already invited Sela to the party and I can't just back out on her now. I know I need to slow things down, but I need to get through the holidays. We've made quite a few plans together."

"I get it," JT says amiably, and claps me on my shoulder. He squeezes once and releases. "But after that, Beck, you should probably cool it a bit with her. You don't want to lose focus on the business, and besides . . . do you really want to be tied down?"

I know I should play along with him, but I can't help a tiny burst of rage over his words. He doesn't know Sela at all. Clearly doesn't have my best interests at heart, because any sane person who saw their friend having the potential for happiness would be seeking instead to encourage it rather than destroy it.

"I said I'd slow it down," I grit out while trying to keep a smile plastered to my face. "But I'm not giving her up. And I'm not averse to being tied down . . . not with the right woman."

"But is Sela really that woman, is all I'm saying, Beck. She's a Sugar Baby. If you want to get tied down, Christ, get my mom to set you up with someone from our circle or something. But she's from Belle Haven, dude. Practically the ghetto."

I have to force myself not to let my hands curl into fists. I have to swallow my anger and smooth out my facial features. I have to hold back the heat in my eyes.

Keep your eyes on the prize, Beck.

Sela's the prize.

"Look, JT," I say slowly, and am pleased to hear my voice is bordering on unaffected. "I hear what you're saying and I'll be careful with her. Right now I'm having fun with a sexy woman. I don't have any designs on getting hitched to her or anything, and I don't forget she's a Sugar Baby. But I'm not done with her yet, okay?"

Not done by a long shot.

JT studies me, considering my words. Finally, he nods with a full smile. "Yeah, sure. I get it, and you're a smart guy. But just know I'm here if you want to talk about her or anything. I'll always have your best interests at heart."

The lie rolls smoothly off my tongue. I give him a playful punch in the chest and tell him, "I've always got your best interests at heart too, buddy. Anything you need, I'm there for you."

. . . .

CHAPTER 15

Sela

"So this is how the other half lives," I whisper to Beck, bumping my shoulder against his as we walk up to the ginormous Pacific Heights mansion owned by his parents, Beckett and Helen North.

"I believe they're called the one percent, not the other half," he says dryly.

"Well, color me impressed," I say softly as I take in the four-story white house with a portico porch held up by massive stone columns.

"The house was built in 1901 in the neoclassical architectural style known as Beaux Arts," Beck says as he sweeps a hand toward his childhood home, "which is epitomized by the flat roof, carved embellishments such as those mascarons above each window, and the numerous and richly detailed balustrades, pilasters, and acroteria that abound."

I stop abruptly and turn to face him with my mouth hanging open.

He grins at me and says, "This house was completely renovated when my parents purchased it before I was even born. What makes it so impressive is how it sits on this hill providing a full and unobstructed 180-degree view of the Golden Gate Bridge, Angel Island, and the San Francisco Bay. You don't even want me to get into the fine appointments inside the house once we go in."

Shaking my head in amusement, I say, "You sound almost proud of this house. You know, the way you just rattled on about the architecture and stuff."

Beck's hand curls around my neck and he pulls me in for a quick kiss. Chuckling, he says, "Nah. Not proud of it at all. I've just heard my mom say those same exact words about a million times as she brags about her house to anyone who will listen, and I picked up a few things."

"That makes sense," I say with a smile as I turn to look at the front decorated with wreaths on every window trimmed in red velvet bows and strategically placed floodlights to light up the façade.

"So you understand the game plan, right?" he asks in a serious voice, almost as if he were a coach and I was his star player.

"Yes," I say with a nod of my head. "Quick in and out. We hunt down your parents for introductions, they can sneer down at me for a few moments, and then you ask to talk to your dad in private. I'll sample all the expensive food, ogle the fancy dresses, and drink a glass of champagne, because . . . well, I love champagne. You finish up with your dad, come grab me, and we jet out of there before anyone can stop us."

"Then we go home and celebrate Christmas Eve together," he adds.

"Preferably naked," I say with an impish grin.

"In front of the fireplace."

"With whipped cream."

"And toys . . . we must play with toys," he says with a laugh, and I can't help but join in. It's funny, because we've both got dirty minds, but it's not funny in the respect that we're both deadly serious about what we just laid out. We now have a date with a fireplace, whipped cream, and sex toys for our Christmas Eve.

"Come on," Beck says as he takes my hand and starts toward the front porch. "Let's get this over and done with."

I follow him up, my heels clicking on the stone steps. Tonight I'm wearing the same dress I wore the night of The Sugar Bowl mixer where JT tried to drug that girl. Beck offered to buy me a new one for tonight's party, but I couldn't see doing that when this one would work. Plus, I knew I looked damn good in it and Beck would appreciate it.

I'm surprised when Beck rings the doorbell of his own childhood home and patiently waits until the massive black iron door done in a scroll pattern and inset with beveled glass is swung open by a butler.

Or a servant.

Or, I don't know what he is, but he's wearing a black tuxedo and makes a slight bow toward Beck. "Good evening, Mr. North. It's lovely to see you."

"Evening, Percy," Beck says to the man, who I'm thinking might actually be a butler. He's older with silvered hair at the temples and has an overt familiarity with Beck in the way that he looks at him right now with a warm smile.

"And whom do you have with you tonight?" Percy asks as he turns my way, hands clasped in front of his stomach and his head tilted at me in curiosity.

"This is Sela Halstead," Beck says, and then adds, "my girlfriend."

Percy's head jerks slightly in surprise and he turns to Beck with a devilish grin. "Well, isn't this a very nice surprise."

Putting his arm around me so he can pull me in closer, Beck presses a kiss to my temple before telling Percy, "She is very nice, I assure you. And not bad to look at, right?"

Percy gives Beck a chastising look and clucks his tongue before turning to me with an apologetic smile. "My apologies for young Beck's impertinence, so let me be the first to say, I'm glad he's found a lovely lady such as yourself."

I blush, hopefully prettily, and I definitely know in this moment he's been around Beck for a good chunk of his life. I'm betting if his parents were as absent as Beck has indicated, maybe Percy was a bit of a father figure to him. I'll have to ask him that later.

"I'll take your coats, and your parents are in the music room the last I saw them," Percy says in what I now recognize as a faint British accent. Shit, they must have imported their butler for maximum effect. "They've been awaiting your arrival."

"We'll head there now," Beck says as we both slip our coats off and hand them over. Beck then takes me by the elbow and starts to lead me past Percy. But then he cranes his head and says to the butler, "Oh, and Percy? You've got a stain on your shirt there. Mother will have a cow if she sees it."

Beck points a finger at Percy's chest and then chuckles when Percy's head snaps downward to look at the offending stain. Of course, his shirt is pristine white, and once he realizes this, his gaze swings up and narrows at Beck.

Beck merely laughs and says, "Gotcha."

I can't help the tiny giggle that pops out as I watch Percy's lips tip up in amusement even as he tries to glare Beck down. I give the older man a tiny wave goodbye and he gives me a warm smile.

We weave in and out of guests, all dressed in expensive finery and jewels, holding crystal flutes of champagne or delicate china plates with ridiculous-looking hors d'oeuvres the size of a postage stamp. Everywhere I look, fresh greenery is draped, and I swear there's a Christmas tree in every room.

Beck nods to some people with smiles but doesn't stop to talk. I know he's on a mission to get this party over and behind us as quickly as possible.

Which makes me wonder out loud, "Why do you even bother to come to this party, Beck? I mean . . . you don't want to be here, don't like your parents very much. Why suffer?"

"Well," he says in a low voice as he inclines his head toward me, but still keeping his gaze forward while we walk to the music room. "First, it's always good to keep your foot in the door somewhat. My father has solid business contacts and I don't want to burn that bridge, but mainly it's to keep them off Caroline's back. They can't stand to have an estranged daughter and how it must look to their friends and peers. So it pacifies them for me to at least step up to the plate and attend a few functions each year. The next will be my father's birthday party."

"If they want to make amends with Caroline, why don't they just do so? End the estrangement?"

Beck laughs sarcastically and squeezes my elbow. "Because, my dear Sela, that would require my parents to apologize for their terrible behavior toward Caroline and Ally, and they would never lower themselves to do so. They just expect her to get over her snit and start acting like a real daughter again."

"I know I've said it before, but I don't like your parents," I mutter.

"The thing that bothers me the most is that they don't seem to care about their granddaughter. She's like this dirty little secret or something," Beck says on a growl, his hand tightening on my elbow reflexively.

Before I can respond, we approach a room with a wide entrance and glass French doors open to either side. I can see why it's the music room, because it's got a large black piano in one corner that I'm guessing cost a mint. It's sparsely furnished with only a couch and two chairs, both done in black leather and sleek contemporary design. The rest of the room is open and clearly designed for parties in mind with plenty of room for people to mingle. But the real focal point is a massive, charcoal-gray marble fireplace that looks like it could hold a football team. A roaring fire is dancing inside, but doesn't seem to be throwing off oppressive heat, so I'm guessing it's flued in such a way to be more for show than anything else.

I can tell the minute Beck locates his parents, because he stands a bit straighter and his hand slips from my elbow to my hand, which he squeezes reflexively. I squeeze back and then we're headed across the room toward a man I easily identify as Beck's father. They share the same dark brown hair, although his dad's is going gray throughout, and brilliant blue eyes. Same facial features, strong jawline. He's his dad through and through. I don't see any resemblance to the tall, elegant blond woman next to him who wears her hair in a sleek bob that comes just a few inches above her shoulders.

As we approach, Beck's mom sees him first and lightly touches her hand to her husband's arm to get his attention. He stops in midsentence, as he was talking to another older couple, and looks down at his wife, then follows her gaze our way. I don't miss that both of them look first to Beck, then drop down to where our hands are clasped, and then over to me in wary interest.

"Beck," his mother says in a light, airy tone of welcome. "So glad you could make it tonight."

Stepping up to his mother, he gives her a light kiss on her cheek. "Mother . . . looking beautiful as ever."

His mother preens with the compliment.

Beck turns to his father and merely nods at him. "Merry Christmas."

"Merry Christmas, Beck," he says in a deep voice, and I'm betting that these two have never hugged in their life.

"And whom have you brought to the party?" his mom asks as she turns her gaze to me in polite interest with a plastic smile on her face.

"This is Sela Halstead," Beck says as he releases my hand and once again wraps his arm around my waist. "My girlfriend. Sela . . . my parents . . . Helen and Beckett North."

I smile, reach my hand out to his mother, and say, "It's a pleasure to meet you Mrs. North."

She takes my hand and gives is a soft shake, still keeping her own smile in place. As soon as she releases it, I offer my hand to Mr. North. His grip is firmer, a complete businessman to the core.

"Mr. North," I say in greeting.

"Well, welcome Sela," Beck's father says before he releases my hand, only to have his mom pounce immediately.

"And where are you from Sela?" Helen North asks me with her chin lifted a little.

"Belle Haven." And I swear, her nose actually wrinkles up a bit. "But I'm working on my master's at Golden Gate University and have an apartment in Oakland."

"She actually lives with me now," Beck says, and I have to wonder why he feels he must antagonize his mother. Even I, who just met his parents not thirty seconds ago, could tell this would not go over well with them.

Well, at least not with his mother.

Helen's eyebrows raise sky-high as she turns to Beck. "Isn't that moving a little fast?"

"I don't know," Beck says smoothly. "You tell me, Mother. I'm assuming you know how long Sela and I have been dating."

His mom just stares at him, completely unable to answer the question. His dad coughs slightly. It was a very pointed reminder from Beck to his parents that they know nothing about him really.

They clearly get the message, because his dad changes the subject quickly. "How's business going?"

"Very well," Beck says, and uses the opportunity to present the real reason we came tonight. "Actually, I need to talk to you about a business issue in private. Do you have some time right now?"

"Beckett," Helen North chides her husband. "It's a party. You're the host. No business tonight."

But I can tell that Beckett North is not only intrigued by his son wanting to discuss business with him, but he'd rather be anywhere but hosting a party tonight. So I'm not surprised when he leans over, pecks his wife on the cheek, and says, "We won't take long, darling. I'm sure you can manage without me for a few minutes."

She huffs out her displeasure as Mr. North steps past us both. Beck leans over, gives my lips a soft brush, and whispers so only I can hear, "Good luck. I won't be too long."

As I watch them walk out of the music room, I see JT across the room. This isn't a surprise, as Beck told me he'd be here and wanted me to be prepared in case we ran into each other. While Beck has done a fantastic job of being buddy-buddy with JT at work this week, I'm not under the same requirement to play nice with him. In fact, Beck and I discussed how I should deal with JT, and we both felt that I should proceed with quiet distaste. Anything else may make him suspicious.

JT is dressed in an elegant navy suit and standing with a couple that look to be in their mid to late fifties. The woman has a sexually charged gaze fixed on Beck's dad as he walks out of the room with his son.

Interesting. I'd bet my bank account, which, granted, isn't much, that I'm looking at JT's mother right now. JT and the man I'm guessing is his father . . . well the man who raised him . . . don't seem to notice where her attention is focused, because they are talking quietly between themselves.

Figuring that I need to make small talk with Beck's mom, I turn her way, only to find her staring at the woman I believe to be JT's mom. Her lips are flattened and her eyes are cold as she watches the other woman staring hungrily at her husband.

Well, that answers that question. Clearly Beck's mom knows about her husband and JT's mom having an affair.

Very strange and complicated people.

"So, Mrs. North," I say in an attempt to get her attention. "Your house is stunning. Beck was telling me a little bit about the architectural style."

Helen's gaze slides slowly to me and her eyes don't warm at all. Rather than prattle on about her home, which Beck sort of assured me was a good conversation maker, she says, "If you'll excuse me, I have some other guests to attend to. Enjoy your evening."

And just like that, I'm dismissed.

I'm immediately relieved that I don't have to engage further with Beck's mom. My low opinion of her was set when I first saw how Helen and Beckett North failed to celebrate the birth of their son, but it sank to unparalleled depths when Beck told me how they treated Caroline after her rape.

A waiter approaches me with a tray of champagne-filled flutes and I gratefully take one, murmuring, "Thank you." I decide to explore the house a bit while I sip on my drink, thus averting the need to talk with any of these people, because really . . . what could we possibly have in common?

I walk out of the music room, back into the main hall. I see people descending a gently curved staircase of a dark wood polished to a brilliant sheen. I follow them down and emerge into what looks to be a large game room complete with a poker table that seats ten and two pool tables that are currently in use. An old-fashioned phonograph sits on an intricately carved table with a cubed glass case over the top, telling me that it's worth quite a bit of money. The walls of the cavernous room are done in rich wood paneling with dark parquet underneath and silk rugs scattered under the furniture. Large, deeply cushioned chairs of mocha-colored leather are clustered in groups with small tables in between. It's a man's room for sure, with not a single feminine touch to be seen.

I casually wind my way through the party guests and stand against a wall that is covered in prints of various golf courses, as well as other golf memorabilia. Sipping at my champagne, I focus my attention on two men playing a game of pool and settle in to wait for Beck to finish up with his dad. I have no doubt that as soon as he's done he'll come looking for me and will eventually find me down here.

"Enjoying the party?" I hear from my left and recognize the voice instantly. Because I don't need to act the part, and because it comes very naturally to me, I turn with cold eyes toward JT as he stands next to me. He's got a glass of a dark-colored liquor in one hand and his other hand tucked causally in his pocket.

He's stares down at me with superiority and amusement, no doubt enjoying his memory of the conversation he had with Beck a few days ago whereby he encouraged Beck to put the brakes on with me. Knowing this man doesn't think very much of me based on the circumstances of my birth, that he's pushing his friend away from a chance at real happiness, and let's not forget that he drugged and raped me, leads me to shut down this nasty conversation before it begins.

"Can't say this is really my speed," I tell him with a slight shrug of my shoulders. My eyes glance around the room before coming back to him. "You know . . . not for a girl from Belle Haven."

"Exactly," he says in what sounds like a polite voice but that's really just to hide his rude declaration that I'm not good enough for this crowd.

This actually amuses me, that he feels the need to tear me down. It also gives me an important piece of information. He's still very worried about my connection with Beck and feels threatened by it.

"But as long as you remember the true role of a Sugar Baby," JT says casually as his gaze flicks from mine to the action on the pool table. He stares at it pensively before continuing, "you should be fine."

"And what role would that be?" I ask sweetly.

"That the arrangement with Beck is temporary and it's a services-only arrangement. You fuck him, he gives you money. It's quite simple, really."

I blink at him, unsure of what to say. Every fiber of my being wants to tell him off and make him understand how close Beck and I truly are, but the part of me that wants him to suffer eventually wins out, so I play it cool. "Thank you for the reminder, Mr. Townsend."

"If you think there's something deeper with Beck, you'd be wrong about that," he insists as he turns back to me. "He doesn't see you as anything more than a great fuck."

If I really wanted to preserve status quo with JT and not alert him to anything, I would meekly agree with his statement. But the fighter in me . . . the woman who hates this man and wants to defend herself to make up for the fact that once I was absolutely defenseless against him, narrows her eyes and sneers, "I *am* a great fuck, JT. A really superb, fantastic fuck. But you and I both know there's more to me than that. Otherwise you wouldn't be trying so hard to tear me down."

JT actually rears backward a bit with eyebrows raised. I can tell he never expected me to fight back.

Before he can even think of a comeback, and before I can ruin anymore of Beck's plan to solidify his friendship with JT so he'll seek him out for money, I step into JT and murmur softly, "But don't worry . . . I would never attempt to come in between your friendship with him. I'm very aware of Beck's feelings for you and I'm going to try to make a very concerted effort to get along with his oldest friend and business partner."

I step back and beam up at him with a warm, brilliant smile. Giving him a nod, I set my half-empty glass down on a small table beside me and say with cheery politeness, "Merry Christmas, Mr. Townsend. It was nice seeing you again."

Stepping past him, I make my way across the billiard room and toward the staircase that leads up. I don't look back at JT, but I can actually feel his confused look pressing in upon me.

. . . .

CHAPTER 16

Beck

I follow my dad out of the music room, across the main hall and to the main staircase. We go up one flight to the next floor that houses his office, the library, media room, and master suite complete with a separate dressing room and his-and-hers master baths. The floor above has four guest rooms plus a home gym and sauna.

My dad's office is as intimidating as it is sumptuous: custom wood paneling with coffered ceilings, a massive crystal chandelier, rare artwork, and a built-in saltwater reef aquarium that takes up one wall. Given that my dad spends most of his time in here, either working his financial advisor magic or probably still fucking JT's mom, I get why he wanted it built to his specific tastes. My gaze slides to the Parnian custom desk made of Carpathian elm and ebony—yeah, the one I hid under while my dad boned Mrs. Townsend all those years ago—that I happen to know was purchased for a cool two hundred thousand dollars because my mom also likes to brag about that as well.

Because we're talking business and my father would never think to sit beside me in one of the two guest chairs made of Macassar ebony and Italian leather, which are as uncomfortable as they look, he takes a seat behind his desk that is so expensive I'm afraid to breathe on it.

When I'm seated opposite him, I don't waste any time getting to the subject. The sooner I get this done, the sooner I can grab Sela and we can start to celebrate Christmas Eve away from this place.

"You loaned JT the start-up capital for The Sugar Bowl," I say simply.

My dad's expression remains neutral, flawlessly composed. "It's no secret. It was a good investment that paid off quickly and lucratively."

"I'm curious if you loaned him the money because it was a good deal or because he's your son."

His reaction is subtle but telltale. A tiny tick in his jaw muscle, and I know I've just made things uncomfortable because we've never discussed this in detail.

My dad, however, recovers quickly and says in an unapologetic voice, "First, because it was a good investment, but also because he's my son."

"Does he know?" I ask quietly.

"That I'm his father?" my dad asks, but doesn't wait for me to reply, merely says, "No. Candace and I felt it was best he not know."

I can actually envision how that conversation went between my dad and JT's mom. Probably something like this.

Candace: *"I'm pregnant, Beckett. And it's yours."*

Beckett: *"How do you know?"*

Candace: *"Because you're the only one who's fucking me."*

Beckett: *"What do you want to do?"*

Candace: *"Keep it, of course. But Colin can't know. He'd divorce me."*

Beckett: *"I understand. That means you'll have to fuck your husband, and soon, so he thinks it's his."*

Candace: *"That sounds like a good plan. We can keep fucking though too, right?"*

Yeah, that's exactly how I bet that conversation went, because I knew all too well that my dad was not going to divorce my mom. He may be a whiz with finances and made his own way in the world of power and money, but my mom comes from old money. The kind that never dies, never goes away. Is infinite and then some.

I also know Candace knows this, and she doesn't come from money. She married Colin after he plucked her out of a Vegas burlesque show. He's fifteen years her senior, obscenely rich, ugly as sin, and dotes on his wife. She's not about to lose that gravy train.

"You and Candace . . . you never thought it was a good idea to let JT know the truth?" I ask, not because I really care for JT's benefit, but because I want to get a read on my dad's feelings, as limited as they may be for his illegitimate son.

"Where are you going with this?" my father counters, evading my direct inquiry. This doesn't surprise me. My dad was never one to talk about feelings and emotion.

I don't answer him directly either, because I can play this game as well. I learned from the best about how to remain detached so I can focus on what's really important. So instead, I say, "I don't begrudge you helping JT with the start-up capital. Hell, that was of benefit to me too."

My dad nods with a smile on his face, utterly relieved I'm not here to give him shit for helping his secret bastard son. But it's time to knock that smile off his face.

"I don't want you to loan him any more money," I say firmly, making sure I hold his gaze, which instantly turns suspicious of me.

"Why?" is all he asks.

"I can't tell you the details. I'm asking you to trust me on this."

Leaning forward to rest his elbows on his desk, he steeples his hands in front of his face and stares at me pensively. Finally, he lowers his hands and asks, "Should I weigh your request to trust you on this with as much consideration as I'd give JT if he came to me and said he really needed the money? Should I trust his need as much as I trust your request? How do I distinguish when you're not giving me any information?"

It's a fair question, to be honest, yet I'm the one who doesn't trust my dad with the details. "Look . . . I don't expect you to distinguish between us as sons. You and I aren't close; I expect no more than you and JT are close. You have a blood tie to us both, and I get that gives you some measure of need to help us out as best you can as a father. But I'm telling you, it would be in your best interest not to give him any more money."

Dad's eyebrows raise in surprise. "You want JT to fail at something, don't you? I'd like to know why."

"I want him to fail at getting a loan from you," I say with a nod. "I'm hoping he'll come to me for the money. I want to be his only resource."

My dad is whip smart, keen, and shrewd. He understands immediately. "You're going to use leverage to buy him out of the company."

"Yes."

"Why?"

My dad doesn't want to know my reasons so he can offer me fatherly advice. He wants to know so he can figure out exactly which son he should align with if it comes down to a choice.

"I can't tell you the details," I maintain. "But I'll just say this . . . JT is not a good man. He's rotten to the core, and trust me when I tell you, there's going to come a time when you're going to regret having him as a son. You'd best start distancing yourself now before you find out exactly how wretched a human being he is."

My father's stoic façade starts to crumble a bit. His brow wrinkles with worry. "If he's in some type of trouble that will bring shame on my name, I need to know—"

I hold up a hand and cut him off. "How can he bring shame on your name? You've never publicly acknowledged him as your son. I suggest you keep it that way."

For this first time since this conversation started, my father looks unbearably uncomfortable. He actually drops his eyes down to his desk, pressing a finger to his temple, which he taps in consternation. I can see he's troubled, and this makes me think that perhaps it's not a well-guarded secret that JT is his son. I can tell by the worry in his eyes that someone else knows, and this worries him.

"Dad," I press him. "Will you do as I ask?"

Sitting back in his chair, my father sighs deeply as he raises his gaze back to me. He seems to be searching for something to say, but I can tell indecision is warring within him.

"I'm telling you, Dad . . . if you believe anything I say, don't give him the money. Things will get very ugly if you do."

"Is that a threat to me?" my dad asks, not in an affronted manner, but with a tired edge to his voice.

"Not at all," I assure him quickly, and then decide to give him just a tiny bit more information to help sway his decision because I need him on board. "I'm telling you JT is bad news. I'm not going to give you details, but I will tell you he's committed a crime that could see him doing serious time in prison. You need to distance yourself from him so you don't get dragged down into the mud. Trust me that I'm trying to do what's best not only for me, but for everyone close to him. But my main interest right now is to get him out of the company before the shit hits the fan, so The Sugar Bowl doesn't suffer because of his mistakes. I'm trying to sever ties from him before this goes down, and I want to make sure you don't have any existing ties as well."

These words hit my father hard. His face sort of sags, turns slightly gray. For the first time in my life, I think he looks old. A tiny stab of pity hits me as I realize that I'm laying some troublesome shit on his doorstep. Then I immediately banish it when I envision the way he and my mother treated Caroline when she was raped.

"I know I haven't been the best father," my dad says as he looks at me with haggard eyes. "But I tried to support you both the only way I knew how, which was financially. I know money better than I know parenting. Maybe if I would have taken more of an interest in JT . . ."

His voice trails off and I can see he's going into pity mode. He's not worried about JT and his demons. He's worried about his own personal failings and how this may reflect upon him. While I don't really care about bolstering his pride, I do need to keep him focused on doing what I need.

"No, Dad," I say firmly. "What's wrong with JT can't be fixed with fatherly love. He's broken, probably on a cellular level. He's broken, no matter what good influences have been around him."

My father's eyes water a tiny bit and he looks at me with un-mitigated hope that perhaps this isn't his fault. That maybe even his defective genes come from Candace, and JT was going to be a screwed-up individual no matter the circumstances.

I can see he needs some type of absolution for being a shitty father to me and an absent father to JT, so I tell him what he needs to hear, regardless of whether it's true or not. "He's broken, Dad. Nothing and no one could have prevented his actions or fix them now. Trust me on that."

Our gazes lock and I give him an encouraging smile.

Finally, he lets out a deep breath of regret and says, "All right. I won't loan him any money if he asks."

I let out my own breath of relief as my hands grip the armrests of the chair. I start to pull myself up, eager to leave now that I have my dad's cooperation. "Thank you."

"Are you in any danger or trouble?" he asks, and that catches me off guard. I don't think I've ever heard him ask me such a question . . . with such genuine concern for my welfare.

"No," I assure him with a smile. "I'm fine. Will be better after I can get JT out of The Sugar Bowl, but I'm good right now. Don't worry."

"Okay," he says quietly, and I start to turn away from him. But then he says, "Does this have anything to do with the young lady you brought with you tonight?"

This also catches me by surprise and I turn back to him. "Why do you ask?"

My father cocks an eyebrow at me. "Beck . . . not once in your ten years of adulthood have you ever brought a girlfriend here. Not only that, I can tell how protective you are of her. And whatever this quest is you are on to sever JT from your life, I think the motivation must be powerful. I'm guessing it's the girl."

My dad will figure out the details soon enough once JT is arrested for Sela's rape, but I'm not about to share that with him. Instead, I merely say, "Everything I do is with the idea in mind of solidifying my future with her."

And for the third time this evening, my father stuns me. He looks at me with admiration and says, "That's a good reason to make a bold move. For love."

I blink at my dad, confused over his words. I didn't think he knew what love was. Hell, I'm not even sure I quite understand it; only that my feelings for Sela are overwhelming to me at the worst of times, and infinitely comforting at the best of times.

Nodding in affirmation to my dad, I merely say, "Merry Christmas. And thank you."

"Merry Christmas, Beck," he says as I turn from him and walk out of his office.

I make my way down the staircase, wondering if Sela stayed in the music room and how horribly my mother may have been treating her. I could see the moment Sela said she was from Belle Haven that my mother's lukewarm curiosity morphed into acute distaste. While I'm sure she doesn't care about my personal happiness, she's very much interested in making sure that I marry the right person and produce socially acceptable grandbabies for her. After all, Caroline did the unthinkable and had a child from the product of rape, and that just wouldn't do for the North family's prestige.

Halfway down the stairs, I see Sela, standing at the bottom, looking up at me with a warm smile. It's like she appeared almost magically, because she was the person I wanted to see the most right then. I level a bright grin at her and trot the rest of the way down.

My arms go around her waist, hers go around my neck, and I plant a deep kiss on her right there, knowing it will set San Francisco gossips on their ears. I vaguely hope my mother is around watching and that she's immensely embarrassed by my behavior.

When my lips pull back from Sela's, she whispers, "I take it the meeting went well?"

"Better than well," I say with a brush of my lips against her temple. Taking her by her hand, I start to pull her to the foyer so

we can leave. "I'll tell you all about it, but we have more important things to do right now."

I see Percy at the entrance, grabbing our coats from the massive closet just off the front door. Sela's hand squeezes mine and
she asks coyly, "Oh yeah, what's so important that we have to do
right now?"

"Don't you remember?" I ask mischievously as we reach Percy.
I take Sela's coat from him first and help her into it. "Whipped
cream and sex toys."

I say this, of course, loud enough for Percy to hear and his ears
turn bright red as Sela looks at me with wide eyes.

"What?" I ask in mock surprise as I grin at her. "You agreed
earlier. Whipped cream and sex toys in front of the Christmas tree
when we got home."

Sela drops her face and snickers. I turn to Percy and take my
coat from him with a jaunty smile. I expect to see condescension
in his expression that I would embarrass him and Sela like that,
but instead his lips are quirked up in amusement even if his ears
are still red.

He turns to Sela and bows slightly. "It was a pleasure meeting
you, Sela. I hope you have a Merry Christmas."

"I hope you do too," Sela tells him warmly as I slip my
coat on.

Impulsively, I reach out and give Percy a hug. A bro-type hug
with a gentle clap on his back. "Merry Christmas, Percy."

"Be well, Beck," he says with misty eyes as he opens the door
for us. "And Merry Christmas."

. . . .

CHAPTER 17

Sela

I wake up slowly, feeling sated, warm, and secure. The sun hasn't quite cracked the horizon, so our room is bathed in a bluish-gray light. I'm lying on my side, my head resting on Beck's bicep as he's spooned around me. His other arm is curled around my waist, large palm fanned out across my stomach. I can tell immediately that he's already awake but just content to quietly hold me.

"Merry Christmas," I say with a rough voice.

His palm presses into my belly and his face nuzzles into the back of my neck. "Merry Christmas. Sleep well?"

I stretch against his hold, testing my muscles.

Yeah . . . I'm sore, and it makes me smile. "Fantastic. You?"

"Best sleep in a long time."

I shift slightly in his arms, which loosen to let me snuggle deeper in his embrace. He pushes a leg between mine, his arms holding tighter once again. Smiling, I murmur, "Last night was—"

"Incredible," he finishes.

So freaking incredible.

When we got back to the condo from his parents' party, we

went at each other like starved animals. A quick raid of the refrigerator revealed quickly enough there was no whipped cream to be had. That didn't dissuade Beck, who tried to pull me to the tiled kitchen floor, but I pushed him off.

"I think there was some talk about toys," I told him. Then I kissed him and bit his lower lip.

He groaned and pushed me away, pointing to the hallway. "Go pick out what you want to play with. Meet me in front of the Christmas tree."

And I knew exactly what I wanted to play with. I knew that the time was right.

When I came back into the living room, I found Beck taking his shirt off while standing in front of the tree. He'd turned all the lights off except for the ones on the tree, and it cast a warm glow across his beautiful body. My mouth went instantly dry and I walked toward him almost in a trance.

When I was no more than two feet from him, I held my hand out and said, "Here. I want to play with this toy."

His gaze dropped to my open palm and his eyebrows raised as he stared at the small glass butt plug and small bottle of lube I was holding. It had been in his bag of toys he'd unceremoniously dumped on the bed beside me a few weeks ago and told me to choose. Back then, I would have never chosen the plug, because when you've experienced the pain and degradation of anal rape, it becomes forbidden territory.

But last night . . . I wasn't scared. Or apprehensive. Or even remotely uneasy about the prospect. Instead, I had an overwhelming need to let Beck take possession of a part of my body that never really belonged to me. It belonged to one of my unknown rapists, and I realized that it was the only part of me left that was still metaphorically unhealed since I met Beck.

He, of course, wasn't as keen on the idea.

He reacted badly, actually. Backed away from me and shook his head. "No, Sela."

"Yes," I insisted. "I want you to."

He opened his mouth to protest. I know it was because he was afraid of hurting me or maybe dredging up terrible memories, but I merely stepped up to him, pushed the objects into his hand, and said, "I trust you."

Beck's face crumbled and his eyes softened, and he took the items from me. He then gave me the most gentle kiss I've ever experienced, and then he proceeded to show me how caring a man can be to a woman.

Thinking about what he did to me . . . my body.

The intense orgasm he wrung out of me while showing me just how pleasing that kind of play can be to a woman.

Beck North claimed that last part of my body as his own with soft words, gentle touches, and a little glass toy that felt as unbelievably good as it felt naughty.

"Want your Christmas present?" he asks as he rubs his stubbled chin over my shoulder, producing a full body shiver.

Hmmmm . . . just thinking about last night. "If it involves you fucking me right now, in this position, then yes . . . I want it very much."

I feel the rumble of laughter in Beck's chest, even as I feel him start to get hard behind me. "That was not the present I was talking about, but I think I can oblige."

And then he does.

His hand slides down from my stomach, right between my legs, where his magical fingers find me wet. They work skillfully, causing my hips to grind back against him, always seeking more with this man.

Knowing he'll give me exactly what I need.

Then he's pushing my outer leg up, sliding his own body

down just a bit, and angling his cock to slip into me from behind. I moan in pure bliss as he fills me up, body and soul.

Beck fucks me slowly as he's spooned around me, the arm that my head is resting on coming up to curve across my chest and hold me tightly. His other hand gripping the back of my thigh firmly to pin me in place. I'm restrained by his strength and the feelings he's causing within me, content to let him leisurely make Christmas morning love to me that is oh so different from the kinky shit we did last night.

He takes me higher and higher, whispering sweet words in my ear, until I fall apart in his arms. He splinters at the same time, groaning deeply his appreciation of the moment that we share.

When the last tremors of our twin orgasms fade, and he drops my leg back down into place, he hugs me tightly, and I have never felt more complete and secure as I do now. Not because of what we just shared, but because my core essence as a human being finally recognizes with complete clarity its other half.

"I think I've fallen in love," I whisper to the sunshine now pouring in through the floor-to-ceiling windows. It seems safer releasing that revelation indirectly, but I can't prevent the words from coming out.

"I hope it's with me," Beck whispers back.

Smiling, I nod my head. "Yeah . . . it's with you."

His arms tighten around me more, nearly to the point of cutting off my breath. I don't care though, because his words fill me with life. "That's fortuitous . . . because I love you too."

I look at Beck carefully, to see if something about him has changed in the last twenty minutes since we just shared the L-word with each other. It was unplanned . . . unscripted and totally unbelievable.

I mean . . . did that just happen?

After a little cuddling, we both cleaned up and dressed in sweatpants and T-shirts. I look at Beck now, with his hair sticking up all over the place and sexy stubble on his jaw and chin, reaching under the tree to pull out the two wrapped presents.

A small box from him is wrapped in silver with a green bow. It looks like a jewelry box and my heartbeat is tripping at the thought.

My gift to him is larger in a flat box about twenty inches square. It's wrapped in rustic brown paper with an old-fashioned Christmas tree design and tied in thin red ribbon that I curled on the ends.

I sit on the couch after setting down my tea and Beck's coffee. He joins me as I cross my legs underneath me, setting the small gift in my hands. Then he sits beside me, kicking his long legs out to rest his feet on the coffee table, resting my gift to him on his lap.

"You first," I say as I nod down at the present he's holding.

"Okay," he responds with a boyish grin, and starts pulling hard on the ribbon. It immediately stretches enough that he can work it free of the corners, and his fingers are tearing into the paper. The brown packing box underneath is nondescript and he glances at me briefly with curiosity. I just smile back and watch as he pulls at the tape securing one end of the box.

Then he's reaching inside and pulling out the picture collage frame that I bought earlier in the week while he was at work. It has a black finish and glass-framed cutouts that provide room for five four-by-six pictures, and it will match the decor of either his home office or the one at Townsend-North.

Turning it over in his hands, his lips curve upward as he studies the photos I'd chosen. Five of us together over the last few weeks. Three of them from Vienna that we had asked locals to take of us. One at an outdoor café where we were bundled in coats, hats, and scarves as we drank Viennese coffee by the Danube. One outside the State Opera House before we went inside, dressed elegantly and Beck's arm around my waist. And one a selfie we'd taken while we waited at the airport for our return flight home. The other two were taken here in San Francisco. One by Caroline at Thanksgiving dinner, when Beck pulled me up from the table and onto his lap after we'd finished eating. He's grinning at the camera and I'm looking slightly embarrassed by his display of affection in front of his sister, but I love this photo because it shows hope in my eyes.

The last photo is a surprise to Beck. He's never seen it before, but I took it lying in his bed one morning while he was still asleep. He was on his back, his face looking so peaceful that I couldn't resist grabbing my iPhone and snuggling in close to him. With my face tilted upward, I placed my lips against his jaw and gave him a soft kiss while he slept.

The picture is magical in my opinion, because it shows not only how beautiful Beck is, but how much I adore him, even when he's not aware of it.

"Sela," he says, his voice a little rough. His fingers brush over the picture of us in bed before looking over at me. "This is amazing. I love it."

Shrugging with my cheeks feeling a little hot, I said, "I thought you could hang it up in one of your offices or something."

"The one at Townsend-North," he says. "As that's where I spend most of my time. That way I can see it more often there."

Pushing the box and wrapping paper off his lap onto the couch beside him, he places the frame on top of it and turns to me. One hand curls around my neck in what has now become to me his classic sign of possessiveness, and it makes me completely gooey inside. He pulls me toward him for a kiss. "Thank you. I'm going to have to say, that's even better than the birthday present you gave me."

I cock an eyebrow at him skeptically.

"It's true," he insists. "Especially because of that photo of you kissing me while I sleep."

Warmth spreads through my chest and my heart thumps over the gratitude in his voice. I press my lips to his briefly before I say, "Merry Christmas, Beck."

"Okay," he says as he pulls away and picks up the small box that was resting on my lap. "Time to open yours."

I take the present from him and shake it slightly. Something inside rattles and I smile slyly. "Wonder what this is?"

Truth be told, the fact that something rattled inside throws me off a bit. I assumed it was jewelry, but whatever is inside is loose and has some substance to it.

"Only one way to find out," he chuckles. "Open it."

My fingers pull at the paper. I'm not one who opens gifts delicately, preferring to tear into them. There's a small white box inside, and when I pull off the top, I gasp in surprise.

Reaching in, I hesitantly pull out what is clearly a car key fob with a Mercedes symbol on it. My thumb rubs the raised silver emblem for just a second before I turn to Beck and say dumbly, "You got me a car?"

He nods enthusiastically. "A GLK350. It's a crossover. Smaller than their other SUVs but very safe. Completely sporty. It's in the garage. Want to go see it?"

"I got you photographs," I say with a thick tongue as my face turns back to the key fob in my hand. "You got me a car."

"Oh no you fucking don't," Beck says as his hand comes to my chin. He grips it and turns me to look at him. "You do not compare the cost of our gifts with each other."

My eyes narrow at him slightly. "You got me a freakin' car, Beck."

"So what? I'm rich," he says calmly.

"I don't need a car," I point out. "I take public transit."

"You can visit your dad more often now," he counters.

"It's a freakin' car—"

"Do you love me?" he butts in.

"Yes," I say, blinking over the change in subject.

"Then do me a favor and graciously accept my gift. And get fucking used to it. I'm going to buy you nice things."

My mouth falls open. I think briefly about continuing to argue, but then I take in the serious look in his eyes that's part exasperation but mostly devotion to me sprinkled with a little bit of excitement to show his care for me in this way.

All of the anger and embarrassment over my paltry gift evaporates and I smile sheepishly as I toss the box and key to the coffee table, and then crawl onto his lap. Looping my arms around his neck, I press a kiss to his stubbled cheek and then pull back to look into his eyes. "Thank you. It's an amazingly extravagant gift, and I'm sorry for my reaction. This will take a little bit of getting used to."

"I intend to spoil you, Sela," he murmurs. "I want to give you the world."

Smiling, I turn my body, pull my arms from around his neck, and curl into him. Resting my head on his shoulder and my palm over his heart, I say, "All I ever wanted was a quiet life. I always thought I'd be alone because of what happened to me. I never thought there was room in my life for anything other than my anger and misery. But now that's all changed. You've already given me the world."

His lips press onto the top of my head and his arms wrap

around me. "Paint a picture for me. What does your world look like with me in it? Tell me where we'll be in, say, a year from now."

"Hmm," I hum low in my throat as I consider his question. "In a small house that sits by the ocean. Maybe a fixer-upper with old linoleum floors we'll want to rip out but they're so charming we leave in, and whitewashed cabinets. We'll have a dog, maybe two, that we can take for walks on the beach. I'll work as a counselor and you'll do programming magic, and when we come home from work, we'll fix dinner together."

"Sounds nice," he says in a low voice as one of his hands strokes my arm.

"And we'll fuck every night, and twice a day on the weekends. We'll listen to bands in dive bars or we'll try out various coffee shops in search of the perfect Viennese cup. Oh, and we'll develop some type of hobby . . . like maybe collecting antiques or something. You know, so we don't get so wrapped up in sex that we never leave the house for very long."

Beck chuckles and squeezes me tight, but then he turns serious. "Do you want kids?"

"I don't know," I answer quickly and honestly, but it's a thought that has plagued me before. "I mean . . . I never thought I'd have a real relationship before, or that I'd even be living with someone and discussing a beach house and dogs. But yeah . . . I like kids. I think I'd be a good mom. I had a great role model, after all."

"Well, I had a crappy role model for a mother," Beck says, not in a bitter way, but more reflective.

"You'd make an amazing father," I say softly. "You're so good with Ally."

"Yeah," he says softly. "I think I would too."

We both fall silent, maybe unsure of what to say after that revelation. I mean, not an hour ago we were declaring our love for the first time, and now we're discussing houses and children. It's too fast and it's overwhelming, and yet it's also a little bit right too. I know this because the ensuing silence as we contemplate this isn't awkward at all.

"So, when this is all over with JT, next on our agenda is to find a small house on a beach somewhere?"

I giggle. "With peeling linoleum floors."

"Got it," Beck says.

Suddenly, I sit up and turn in his lap to look at him, reality seeping back in to our discussion of happily-ever-after dreams. "What if this doesn't work? So many things could go wrong. Van-Zant may not take the offer, then we'd depend on fate for him to lose. Or he could go to the police and tell him about the bribery—"

"We're shielded from that," Beck reminds me quickly. "Dennis said there won't be any ties to us. It's why we're paying him so much."

I disregard those assurances, because here's the really big "if." "We still have to depend on JT coming to you for the money."

"Well, he can only go to me or my dad," Beck points out. He relayed to me the entire conversation he had with his dad on the drive home last night, and it does seem his dad is on board with us. "JT doesn't have any other close friends with this type of liquid cash to help him out and no bank will loan him money to pay off a debt. Dennis assured me the collection deadline will be short so he'll be under pressure to act fast."

"Maybe JT won't agree to give up the company for your loan," I offer, even though we've hashed this all out before. "Maybe he'll opt for a beating. Or take his chances elsewhere. Or even negotiate an extension."

"Then worst-case scenario, he's still part of the company when we go to the police," Beck says firmly. I know he's frustrated over my continued worries, but he's also very patient with me.

"It will kill The Sugar Bowl." The bitterness is evident in my voice. "It could ruin you. Maybe we shouldn't even do this at all."

"What?" Beck exclaims, his eyebrows rising high. "You want me to just stay with JT as a partner and pretend none of this happened?"

"No," I say sullenly, my gaze dropping from his. I twist my fingers together and mutter. "I know you could never do that."

"Sela," Beck says softly, his fingers tilting my chin up. When my eyes lock on his, he gives me a knowing smile. "I'm not going to lie . . . I've got a lot tied up in this business. I'm proud of it. It's lucrative. But it is not my only idea. My entire self-worth isn't dependent on it. My financial stability most certainly isn't, as I've invested well and I could buy us houses on multiple beaches and we'd never have to work again a day in our lives. Worst fucking case, I can't get JT out and the police won't compel him for DNA and he stays free. If that happens, then we'll move to a faraway beach and start all over again."

Tears suddenly fill my eyes as quickly as the blossoming love in my heart starts to overwhelm me. This man . . . that he would do that for me?

Beck tilts his head to the side, his smile turning softer, and he wipes a stray tear that runs down my cheek. "I fell hard for you, Sela. I'm committed to *you* and *our* future."

"So this is love?" I whisper hoarsely as I stare into his beautiful eyes.

"I do believe it is," he tells me with a grin. "Now . . . would you like to go see your new car, Miss Halstead?"

I can't help it. His attitude is infectious, and I grin back at him before backing off his lap and dropping to my knees before him.

Placing one palm on each knee, I nudge his legs apart. "Why Mr. North, I would love to, but first I really would love to suck your cock."

"Christ," Beck mutters as his head drops back onto the cushion of the couch and he sighs with happiness. "If you must."

"Oh, I must."

CHAPTER 18

. . . .

Beck

"I'm really sorry JT couldn't make this meeting," I say as I shake hands first with Michael Gruber, then with Vincent Carmon, the two owners of ET Technologies.

"No problem," Vincent responds with an affable smile. He's the younger of the two entrepreneurs, having recently turned twenty-two. Michael's not much older at twenty-three.

"We really wanted your eyes on this project anyway," Michael adds. "We just don't have your programming skills."

It's true enough. They would need me on this project, and I'm very much interested. ET Technologies was founded by Michael and Vincent, college buddies who dreamed up the potential to analyze facial expressions of consumers reacting to certain products. The "ET" part of their name actually stands for eye twitch, a comical play on a common facial expression to indicate unease.

JT had hit me up several weeks ago about this company, as they were looking for not only start-up capital but help with the coding and programming. They approached Townsend-North, and after analyzing their proposal, we finally had been able to set up this meeting. Of course, JT was supposed to be here, but he was a no-show, and this is both a relief and a worry.

I worry because the Mariota-VanZant fight is in five days and our plan is in full swing. VanZant accepted the payoff to take a dive, and according to Dennis, wasn't plagued by any doubt over his decision. Seems he's been nursing a rotator cuff injury that has been kept in absolute secrecy so as not to disturb the odds, and had doubts about being able to take down Mariota anyway. This offer was opportune, as it gives him financial stability and he can later reveal the injury that may help explain the loss and give him a future shot at a big title fight.

So because the plan has been officially enacted, and we are one step closer to stringing up JT by his balls, I don't want anything to fuck this up. JT normally isn't one to miss business meetings unless he's partying hard. And thus is my worry . . . that perhaps he's gone on a bender, which leaves him unpredictable. I can just see the fucker getting a wild hair up his ass and deciding to change his bet over to Mariota or something.

But I've got more important things to pay attention to at the moment.

"Like I said," I tell both men as I walk them out of my office, which is where we had been meeting for their formal pitch to Townsend-North. "I'm very interested in the project. I'd like a few weeks to go over all of the materials and talk to JT about it, but I think we can do something for you."

Both men's eyes light up, as they can start to see their hard work and amazing ideas have a fighting chance in the competitive world of tech industry. What they don't know is that I have no intention of discussing this with JT. My hope is that by this time next week, he's going to be begging me for money and quickly on his way out of my life. Then I fully intend to work with these two men—both geniuses really—and help them bring this advanced technology to life.

Linda stands from her desk as we emerge from my office. We exchange brief farewell formalities and she walks them back up to the lobby for me. Now that the only meeting I had scheduled for the day is over, I have another appointment outside of the office. It's more important than this meeting I just had, will take much longer, but the results will be worth it. Looking at my watch, I see I have just enough time to check my emails before I have to leave, and also put in a call to Dennis. I want to know if he knows what JT is up to. He might still be watching him for all I know, and I don't have time to figure out what my partner is up to this week. I would just like some assurances that he's not going off the deep end before we can attempt to get him out of The Sugar Bowl.

It's later than I had hoped when I get to the condo. I'd sent Sela a text to go ahead and eat without me since my appointment ran over, but it couldn't be helped.

After closing the door behind me and setting my keys on the foyer table, I call out, "Sela?"

"Back here," I hear from our bedroom.

Smiling, I make my way to her, eager to reveal the results of my appointment today. When I step into our bedroom, I'm momentarily stunned when I see a blond woman standing there, facing me with a tentative smile on her face. For a second, I think Sela must have a friend visiting, but then I instantly recognize those blue eyes. I immediately recognize that body that belongs to me.

All at once, my soul recognizes its mate.

"Surprise," she says softly with a flick of her hands to her hair.

It's still long and styled in loose waves, but it's now golden blond with subtle lighter streaks mixed in. It's so different, and yet . . . it's absolutely Sela.

It's Sela in all of her natural beauty, and I'm dazzled.

I walk to her slowly, my eyes roving over her hair that she obviously had lightened today. After I found out about JT, Sela had told me that she colored her hair dark hoping JT wouldn't recognize her. Back then, I couldn't imagine her as a blonde, since I'd only known her as a brunette, but now that I see it . . . it's the way she's supposed to be.

"It's not my exact natural shade of blond," she says softly, her eyes looking at me with undisguised need for approval. "But it's close enough."

I reach out, take a lock resting over her shoulders, and lift it for closer inspection. Then I slide my eyes to her and say, "I love it. You're stunning."

"I wanted to get back to being me, you know?"

"And now you are," I assure her as my arms wrap around her waist to pull her in close.

"Do you like it?"

"I love it, Sela. But your hair could be bright orange and lime green, and I'd love that too on you."

She laughs, pushing her face into my neck, where she kisses me lightly. I tighten my hold on her, enjoying the security and warmth of nothing more simple than a hug from her right now.

"I have something to show you too," I tell her.

Sela relaxes her grip on me and tilts her head back to look at me questioningly. I release her and take a step back, my hands going down to the hem of my sweater. I grab it along with the T-shirt I'd been wearing underneath and pull them both up and over my head.

"If this is some ploy to get me in your bed, Mr. North," she says playfully and with just enough heat in her eyes that I know she likes what she sees, "then all you had to do was ask."

"I intend to have you in that bed," I tell her ominously as I drop my clothes to the floor. "But I need to show you something first."

She tilts her head curiously as I turn away from her, showing her my back. I hear a tiny gasp from her as she whispers, "Oh."

"I'll need you to peel off the bandage," I tell her, eager to show her the new tattoo on the back of my right shoulder.

There's no hesitation as her fingers gently tug at the adhesive tape around the edges. "You got the phoenix covered?" she whispers.

"Well, I started the process of getting it covered, but it will take a few sessions. Didn't want you to see it anymore. Couldn't stand the thought of it being on my body. Not after knowing what it means to you."

I can feel the bandage pull free. She doesn't touch the new artwork, but she must be peering at it closely, because I can feel her breath against my skin. She's silent for a moment as she studies it, and I can't imagine what's going through her mind as she looks at the massive green and black dragon that will eventually obliterate the phoenix. There was no particular significance of that mythical animal other than I thought it looked fierce and protective, which seems to be my underlying motive these days for all my actions. And while it's going to take a few sessions to complete the detail work on the tattoo, it's blurring the phoenix nicely for the time being.

I wait for her to peruse it, because the detail of what has been done is amazing, and I can tell when she finally sees her name by her sharp intake of breath.

The tattoo artist worked mostly on the top of the dragon for this session, while outlining in the rest. Its neck is curved, the head rearing back and mouth open with a stream of red, yellow, and orange fire shooting forth. Within the flames, the artist wrote Sela's name in delicate black script.

She doesn't say anything, so I turn to face her. Her beautiful blue eyes are shimmering with tears and she hastily blinks them clear.

"You like?" I ask with a light smile, wanting to remove the heaviness surrounding us.

"I love it," she says softly. "But you didn't have to do that. That phoenix on your shoulder meant nothing to me."

"Maybe not," I tell her. "But it meant something to me. Something bad, and I wanted it gone."

Sela's lips curve upward and she presses in closer to me, face still tilted so our eyes don't lose connection. "Don't you find it interesting that both of us went out today in secret and made major changes in our appearance? And we did it in secret because we wanted it to be a surprise to the other person?"

"It just means great minds think alike," I say with a laugh, my hands going to the bottom of her sweatshirt to pull it up and over her head. Once it clears, I tell her, "Now let's get naked. I want to do dirty things to you."

"Maybe I want to do dirty things to you," she counters with a wink, her fingers working at the button and zipper to her jeans, even as she kicks her shoes off.

"That would require me to lay on my back, and can't do that with the fresh tattoo," I say.

"You could just stand there while I drop to my knees," she says playfully as she sheds her jeans.

And, oh Christ . . . the thought of that.

Shaking my head, I give her a chastising look as I take my own jeans off. "I called dibs on being the hander-outer of dirty things."

"'Hander-outer?'" she laughs.

"Shut up," I mutter affectionately. "And lose the bra and panties while you're at it."

When we're both naked, Sela crawls into the middle of our bed and I follow right behind her, pausing only halfway up her body so I can work her pussy with my tongue. Sela is so responsive to me—has given me her trust—that it never takes me long to bring her to climax if I hit her hard. But now I take my time, swirling my tongue in leisurely strokes against her flesh. I open my ears and hear her breathing get faster and faster. Her moans start out soft but get deeper the closer she gets. When I back off her clit, she groans in frustration and moves her hands to my head, trying in vain to push my mouth onto the exact spot she needs me to lick before she'll come.

I tease her mercilessly, not because I want her to suffer, but because I know it feels good to her. I also want to show her that I love this place on her body so much I'm content to just lie here on this side of forever as long as she's loving what I'm doing to her.

"Let me come," Sela whispers to me, her hips now gyrating wildly under me. "Please, Beck."

Smart girl. She knows I can't resist her begging.

Fluttering my tongue over her sensitive clit, I press two fingers deep inside her and curl them upward. Sela's back arches and she cries out, "Yes!" as she explodes against my mouth.

"Mmm," I hum against her, laving her softly with my tongue as she starts to fall back down to earth. "That was beautiful."

"Fuck me," she pants as she raises her head to look down at me blearily. "Now."

And goddamn . . . I love that blond hair. It's Sela, but she's different. Softer. More innocent looking, more like her deepest self that remains untouched by the horror she suffered.

I push up, place my hands on Sela's hips, and flip her onto her stomach. I know she wants a hard fucking, because she always does when I drag out her first orgasm. I also know that this position drives her absolutely crazy with lust, so I pull her hips up off the bed, take my cock in hand, and shove it into her without preamble.

"Oh fuck, that's good," I mutter as Sela grunts out her approval, her back arching once again from the pleasure of my invasion.

I pull out slowly, looking at Sela's blond hair spilling down her back, hanging over her shoulders. Reaching out, I grab a hunk of it with one hand, twist it until it loops once around my hand, and give a tiny tug. Her head pulls upward before tilting to the side where I can see a lazy smile on her face.

I slam back into her and she lets out a long groan. "Like that?" I ask her gruffly.

"Mmm-hmm," she purrs low in her throat. "Again."

With one hand at her hip and the other wrapped in her beautiful hair, I start to fuck her hard and fast. Withdrawing to the tip, ramming back in deep. Sela attempts to participate by pulling away and adding her own push backward, but I hold her tight by her hair and hips, making her stay still so she takes what I give her.

I once may have been worried restraining Sela in any way would be too frightening, but I have to accept that she's given me her trust along with her love, and that she's secure in the knowledge that I will only ever bring her pleasure.

Moving in and out of this woman, listening to her sounds and smelling sex in the air, knowing how she feels for me and I feel for her . . . there's nothing comparable to this feeling. So I continue to fuck her hard, holding her in place, and watch for the signs that Sela will come again for me.

I've learned them well.

Her fingers grip the bedcovers, she sucks in a long, deep

breath, and a tangible stillness overcomes her for just a moment. I slam in hard, urging her release, and she gives it to me with a cry and another deep arching of her back. Her pussy clamps hard on to my cock and it causes my own orgasm to rip free.

"Jesus . . . that feels good," I groan as I press my pelvis to her ass and grind it out against her. She grinds right back against me, intent on drawing it out for both of us as long as possible until we fall into a jellylike pile of limbs onto the mattress.

I immediately wrap my arms around her waist and roll us to our left sides so I can spoon against her without banging my tattoo on the covers. Our breathing is choppy and our skin is wet with sweat, both indications of some amazing fucking.

But then again, with Sela, it's always amazing.

Her fingers stroke my forearm as she starts to settle. "So . . . you like the blond hair?"

"Love it," I tell her honestly. "You look so different, but still you. Very hot."

She chuckles, wiggles against my body to get closer to me. We enjoy the silence until a thought strikes me.

"I wonder if JT would recognize you now?" I ask her.

"I wondered that too," she says quietly. "It's been ten years."

"My gut says he wouldn't, because he's so self-centered and narcissistic, he probably doesn't even notice the appearance of the women he preys upon. I know this sounds bad, but I don't think he cares enough to notice much."

"I thought the same thing too when I had decided to color my hair. I didn't want to do it, but I didn't want to take any chances either. But still . . . my gut said he wouldn't recognize me."

"Still," I muse, "it's best we keep you two apart. On the off chance he would, I don't want him having any inkling we're on to him. Taking him down with surprise is going to be key."

"Agreed," she says softly. "And besides . . . we don't have much longer until this all starts heating up."

That's true. In five days VanZant should take a dive. Dennis says JT's bookie is poised to collect hard and fast, because he knows JT could be a flight risk with those stakes. I figure by the middle of next week, JT will be paying me a visit to ask for money.

And if not, then Sela and I will be at the police station, reporting her rape, and we'll let the chips fall where they may.

. . . .

CHAPTER 19

Sela

It's fight night and I've somehow slipped into hostess mode for the men. I've never entertained before. Cooking Thanksgiving dinner for Beck, Caroline, and Ally was my first and only attempt at playing Martha Stewart. I was terrified, mostly because I wanted Caroline to like me, but it all ended up being fine. So when Beck told me he invited Dennis over to watch the Mariota-VanZant fight with us, I immediately decided we would need snacks and alcohol.

I spent the morning at the grocery store and bought enough food to feed an army. My menu consisted of sweet-and-spicy meatballs, buffalo chicken dip and little ham-and-cheese sliders. My afternoon consisted of making these snacks and batting Beck's hands away when he tried to taste.

I then focused on making Devil's Brew, a secret punch handed down through the generations of the Halstead family. I had to call my dad for the recipe, as I'd never made it before, but it was pretty simple: brut champagne, vodka, brandy, frozen limeade, maraschino cherries, and ginger ale. Mix it all up and prepare for your worries to melt away. I thought it was important to have a concoction like this because frankly, until I saw VanZant take the dive, I was going to be stressing out about it.

Dennis came over at five o'clock when the prefights started, lesser-ranked MMA fighters hoping for their chance at fame and fortune. This was opportune, because it let me get acquainted with the sport and Dennis and Beck explained things to me as best they could. While both men sneered at my Devil's Brew, once they heard it had champagne in it, they tried it. By the third glass, they were mellow and happy and waging personal bets on the fighters, yelling at the TV and high-fiving each other when something amazing happened.

I liked hanging with Beck and Dennis. It was fun watching them have a good time, given the heavy nature of the fight that was about to come. I was enjoying everything myself until about 8:30 P.M. when Mariota and VanZant were brought into the cage.

The fighters went at it in an octagonal cage bordered with vinyl-coated chain-link fence, which lent a sinister air to the match. I'd learned quite a bit watching the early fights, including some of the rules. Dennis told me when the Ultimate Fighting Championship was first created, there were very few rules in place to ensure the safety of the combatants. But over time and in an effort to legitimize the sport, rules had been enacted to help prevent serious injury or even death. That didn't mean there still weren't serious injuries though. In the ten preliminary fights before the main event, every fight ended with either a knockout—where one fighter was knocked unconscious—or a technical knockout, where the ref intervened and stopped the fight based on his opinion a fighter could not continue. It's a vicious sport where the blood flows freely. So freely, in fact, that by the time Mariota and VanZant enter the octagon, there's blood smeared over most of the flooring, and I have to wonder what possesses men to get in the ring to do that, especially when the pay isn't all that great for most of them.

"Anyone want a refill on something?" I ask the men before I sit down on the couch beside Beck. They both look at me and shake their heads, eyes going immediately back to the TV screen as the fighters are being announced.

Mariota is shredded, rocking a tattoo-covered eight-pack and a shortly trimmed Mohawk. Most men tonight had closely cropped hair or shaved heads so that their opponents couldn't grip their head that way. VanZant looks slightly bigger than his opponent, as he was in a higher weight class before he dropped down, but he doesn't seem as chiseled. Having watched the other fights, however, I also know this means nothing. In those fights, it seemed to boil down to speed and skill, with many knockouts, technical or otherwise, happening when one opponent went to the mat and the other straddled him, landing a flurry of quick blows to the head, or sometimes just a fast, well-placed kick to the head.

Taking my seat next to Beck, I can't help but mimic his and Dennis' posture. Both on the edge of their seats, legs slightly spread, elbows resting on knees. Hands clasped tightly and intense focus on the TV screen. We're all nervous as hell right now, wondering if VanZant will go through with his commitment to take the dive. I have to think that JT is watching the fight right now, with probably the same nervousness. Or hell . . . perhaps he's enjoying this moment, the type of addictive personality that enjoys the euphoria of the gamble and the possibility of a big win.

"What round do you think he'll go down in?" I murmur to no one in particular.

"He'll take it all the way," Dennis says. "To preserve his credibility for future fights. I'm guessing late in the last round."

I'd learned tonight that there are five rounds, five minutes each, and those few fights that went the distance, both fighters were huffing and puffing hard near the end.

"Makes sense," Beck says as the announcer introduces the fighters to the crowd and the millions watching on TV. It doesn't appear there's a favorite, the crowd equally cheering for both men when announced.

A few more minutes of the fighters meeting in the middle of the ring for the ref to go over the rules, and then the bell rings for round one to start.

My heart is practically in my throat as they come at each other warily, circling and pawing the air with hands protected with fingerless gloves. Testing each other out, I learned. Waiting to see who would make the first move.

I vaguely hear the announcers on TV discussing VanZant: *"He's been criticized a bit about being a counterfighter, so I think we'll see him try to disprove that by coming out strong . . ."*

Mariota makes a short, quick lunge at VanZant, looking like he's going to throw a cross. VanZant's hands come up higher to protect his face, only to take a sharp kick to his ribs. It doesn't seem to hurt him though, because VanZant moves in closer and throws a volley of punches left and right to Mariota, who now goes on the defensive by moving back across the ring and covering his head with his hands.

"See, that's exactly what I expected," one of the announcers says. *"VanZant wants to put Mariota on the defensive right away. Let him know he's not just going to counter his moves."*

VanZant backs his opponent right up to the chain-link fence and continues to throw jabs, crosses, and hooks, these punches I learned quickly enough with Dennis' explanations during the first fights. My heart now feels like it's going to explode out of my chest as VanZant seems intent on pounding the ever-loving shit out of the other man.

"He's not going to take the fall," I whisper fearfully.

Beck reaches over, grabs my hand, and squeezes hard as he keeps his gaze glued onto the TV.

I see our plan going down the drain and JT becoming two million dollars richer, and I'm stunned that just in a matter of thirty seconds, it appears our plan is being derailed.

With a mighty heave, Mariota manages to push VanZant back a few feet. He's been cut over his left eyebrow and blood pours freely down his face. Both men take a short breather, circle each other, and then in a move so fast I'm not even sure I really understand what happens. Mariota spins 360 degrees, leaps into the air, and launches a kick to the side of VanZant's head.

Almost as if in slow motion, I see his head snap to the side and his eyes roll backward before his legs buckle and give way to gravity.

"Oh, look at that tornado kick Mariota just landed," the announcer screams above the roaring crowd. *"And VanZant is down."*

As I've come to find out is typical in these fights, just because your opponent goes down doesn't mean the fight is over. Mariota leaps onto VanZant's prone body, straddles his waist, and starts raining down blows to his head. But almost just as quickly, the ref is there, grabbing Mariota by the waist and pulling him off. It's the universal sign that the ref just declared a knockout.

"It is all over for VanZant," the other announcer says with unfettered awe in his voice. *"Just unbelievable. What has been billed as a match that would go all five rounds has been settled in just thirty-seven seconds with a crushing kick by Mariota to VanZant's head. I don't think anyone predicted this would happen . . ."*

My head turns slowly toward Beck. He turns to meet my gaze, his mouth slightly open in astonishment.

"Did that just fucking happen?" he mutters.

"Jesus Christ," Dennis says in disbelief.

"I don't think that was a dive," I say, my head turning back to the TV as I watch a doctor enter the ring and attend VanZant, who seems to be conscious but completely disoriented. Mariota runs around the octagon, flexing his muscles and screaming victory at the crowd. "I think Mariota caught him off guard."

"Doesn't matter if it was a dive or not," Beck says. "I'll pay him the money."

We all three watch as VanZant is helped onto wobbly legs and led out of the ring. Mariota retains his title belt and holds it up proudly for all to see.

And somewhere, probably in his own house, JT is probably watching in horror as he tries to figure out how he can come up with four million dollars.

I let out a small snort of euphoria. A horrible sound, really, causing both Beck and Dennis to look at me. I immediately clap my hand over my mouth in embarrassment, but then another one pushes forth. They stare at me with wide eyes, and then I start laughing hysterically, pulling my hand away so I can let it all out. I double over at my waist, slap Beck on his thigh with my palm, and laugh until I wheeze.

Beck puts a hand on my back and chuckles as he rubs.

"Holy shit," I gasp as I sit back up straight again, wiping tears from my eyes with the back of my hand. "That was intense. I thought for sure during those first few seconds that VanZant was going to knock Mariota out."

"Me too," Beck says with a grin.

"Un-fucking-believable," Dennis adds, then stands up from the chair. "And this definitely calls for a celebration."

He picks up our empty glasses and heads into the kitchen, presumably to refill our glasses with more Devil's Brew. Beck and I sit in silence, still somewhat stunned that VanZant lost. I mean . . . we wanted him to lose. We expected him to lose, since he said he would, but there was always that strong fear it wouldn't happen.

Dennis returns in a minute balancing three highball glasses between his big hands. He pauses at the couch, and Beck and I carefully each take a glass from him, not really caring who's is whose. Beck and I have traded bodily fluids enough, and there's enough of a buzz going on that I don't care if I drink after Dennis either.

"Looks like I'll be visiting Mr. VanZant with some money," Dennis says as he sits back down in his chair. Gone is the excited posture with his ass hanging off the edge of the seat. Now he's settled back in with one leg casually propped on the other. He didn't wear a suit tonight, for which I was thankful. In his jeans and a faded Chicago Bears sweatshirt, he looks just like an average joe hanging out with friends on a Saturday night. It makes him seem more approachable, and the air of mystery he seems to have around him is dispelled a bit.

I'm not sure how Dennis is going to get five hundred thousand dollars in cash to VanZant. I know he's got the money, because he cashed the check Beck had given him, but you just can't take that much money out of a bank and not call attention to yourself. But then again, I don't need to be worrying about those specifics. It's why Dennis had us give him the money to launder before passing it on to VanZant. Plausible deniability is what he called it.

"JT has to be shitting his pants right now," Dennis muses with an evil laugh. And I like that laugh. Like how much that Dennis has taken such a vested interest in helping me get justice. It's nice to know someone besides Beck cares.

"So what will happen now?" I ask.

Dennis takes a gulp of his drink, smacks his lips, and tells me, "The bookie is likely sending JT some type of message right now. Probably a phone call to make arrangements for payment. He'll give JT a deadline, and I have it straight from the horse's mouth he's only giving him twenty-four hours."

"Is that normal?" Beck asks.

Dennis shrugs. "I think in this case, and with him doubling down that type of money, it was made clear to JT when he placed the bet that they expected immediate payment if he lost."

"And what if he doesn't pay?" I sit forward on the couch a bit, eager to hear this next part.

"I expect they'll impress upon him the urgency of paying," Dennis says ominously, and I'm sort of surprised he doesn't rub his hands together with glee while giving an evil *mwah-ha-ha-haaa* laugh.

Hell, I want to laugh like that at the prospect of JT getting beaten up for failure to pay his debts. It's almost as good a fantasy as when I imagine him in prison getting his ass raped by some beefy dude who will make him his bitch.

As if he can read my thoughts, Dennis says, "It will hurt, Sela. Trust me."

"Think they'll videotape it for me?" I ask with a grin.

Dennis and Beck both laugh, and I realize that all the tension we were all feeling just five minutes ago has left the room. We're now almost delirious with excitement over how the plan will progress next.

"I just hope the ass whupping is enough to impress upon him the dire situation he's put himself in. He's got to be desperate when he comes to me," Beck says.

"He will be," I say confidently, my hand going to the back of Beck's neck, which I squeeze slightly for reassurance. I'm feeling good about this now. Really good.

"Listen . . . I went ahead and pulled the investigative file of your rape from Santa Clara," Dennis says to me in an abrupt change of subject. My eyes slide from Beck to his. "They did a pretty good job from what I could tell. Scoured cab companies; interviewed people at the mall who may have seen you and the other boys who gave you the ride. But as you know, they didn't get any solid leads."

I nod, because this isn't news to me. While my parents kept me shielded from actually dealing with the lead criminal investigator, they did keep me updated. Ultimately, the failure to find who did it caused me to tailspin and landed me in the hospital again. It was my second admission because of JT.

"I also wanted to see if there was anything in there that maybe they missed," Dennis adds.

"I assume there wasn't," Beck surmises. Because otherwise he would have told us the minute he arrived tonight.

"Nothing I could see they failed to do," Dennis says. "But I did see something that was interesting. I couldn't find any paperwork where the DNA lab that ran the semen sample submitted the results to NDIS."

"NDIS?" I ask in confusion.

"The National DNA Index System," Dennis tells me. "It's part of the FBI Combined DNA Index System database that all law-enforcement agencies in the nation submit DNA results to. It should have been done in your case."

"But it wouldn't have helped anything," Beck points out. "JT's never been arrested, so he wouldn't be in the system."

"True," Dennis agrees. "But I still reached out to the lab to see about getting a copy of the paperwork. That way we'll have a complete copy of the file. Just making sure all the t's are crossed and i's dotted so when you report JT, you know exactly what the police know."

"Thank you," I say softly while looking at Dennis. "I'm just so grateful for what you've done for me. I don't even know how to show you how much it means."

Dennis' face flushes red and he ducks his head to take another sip of his drink. He mumbles, "Well . . . you're a sweet girl. I want that fucker to pay."

Beck shoots me a smile and I can see he's equally as touched that Dennis seems to go above and beyond for us. And because he seems loose and relaxed, and even like . . . a friend, and because I'm also buzzed, I ask him teasingly, "So how do you know so much about the seedy underworld? Bookies, and taking dives and bribes. You seem so normal and . . . I don't know . . . like too suave to know about that stuff."

He doesn't answer right away, but stares reflectively into his glass. Then he tilts it to his mouth and drains it, and I know he's got to be feeling the effects by now. When his gaze lifts back up to mine, I'm taken aback to see them flooded with pain and anger. "I was very much a part of that world for a while. Married into it, actually."

"Oh," I say on a small gasp, not shocked by his revelation because he wears a wedding ring, but by the anguish I still see on his face. And although I know it's nosy, I can't help but try to appease my curiosity, since he's opened the door and become infinitely more interesting to me than he was just five seconds ago. "Is her family mob or something?"

"Close enough," Dennis says, and starts to lift his glass again to his mouth before realizing it's empty. He frowns and stands. "I'm going to get another drink. Want one?"

Beck shakes his head and Dennis turns to the kitchen, but I continue to pry, because just . . . wow. Dennis married into the mob?

"You should have brought your wife tonight," I say impulsively. Because I like Dennis and I'm betting I'd like his wife too. I know Beck likes Dennis . . . they've formed an easy friendship these last few weeks. I mean . . . maybe we could all double-date or something.

"She's dead," Dennis says softly, and his eyes actually shimmer with kindness over my suggestion. "Three years ago."

"Oh God," I say, my hand coming to my chest, where I rub at the dull ache that's appeared. "I'm so sorry. That was so insensitive of me—"

Dennis holds his hand up to cut me off, even as Beck's hand goes to my lower back to soothe me. "It's fine, but I suppose this is relevant to why I'm helping you. She was killed as a vendetta against her father. It's a dangerous life and she suffered for it."

"You suffered for it," I whisper.

Dennis nods with a sad smile. "Yeah . . . I did. Lost the most precious thing in my life. The only way out of that life is through death, and when Rosa was killed, it released me from the family as well. But I still have contacts and ties that I used to help you. I also understand vengeance and the need for justice."

"Was her killer brought to justice?" I ask, because I have to know. "Is he in jail?"

"No," Dennis says, even though light shines from his eyes. A light that shimmers and sparkles with satisfaction and pleasure. "He's not in jail, but justice was served."

A tiny shiver runs up my spine over his words as I understand their meaning. I nod at him in solidarity, because now I know that Dennis and I share something very much in common. We both believe that death is an appropriate sentence for someone that would dare to hurt either of us. While that might not be my ultimate goal anymore, it's nice to know that I'm not the only one who fantasizes about murder as the best means of retribution.

As much as I care for Beck and know how much he feels for me, I know now that Dennis is probably the only one who would truly understand what my initial motivations were, and how hard it was for me to give up that quest to kill JT so that I could have peace.

. . . .

CHAPTER 20

Beck

I knew it would happen sometime soon, but just not this soon. Sunday afternoon, less than sixteen hours after VanZant lost to Mariota, JT called me.

From the hospital. Sela and I were actually cleaning up the condo and putting the Christmas decorations away. When I saw JT's name on my caller ID, I didn't think that he'd be calling me about the money he owed. It was too soon for anything major to happen, but I was instantly alerted to what this was really all about when he said in a rough but weakened voice, "Beck . . . I'm at Marin General in Greenbrae. I need you to come get me."

"What happened?" I asked with as much fake concern as I could muster.

"Not now . . . just come get me. They won't release me until someone can drive me home."

"I'm leaving now," I told him, then hung up the phone.

Sela had been on the living room floor, looking as lovely as she ever has in a pair of worn sweatpants and a tattered T-shirt; no makeup and hair in a messy ponytail. She stared at me with knowing eyes.

"JT's in the hospital over in Greenbrae," was all I said.

"Holy shit," she murmured in amazement, because like me, she didn't think it would happen that fast.

"This is it," I told her, and she grinned back at me.

Marin General sits only seventeen or so miles from my condo, but it takes me almost forty minutes to make the drive, given the slow Sunday traffic in the city and across the Golden Gate. At the information desk, I'm directed back to the emergency bay, where I find JT sitting on a hospital bed in a curtained room.

And while I knew that JT was going to be getting a message from the people who wanted their money, I wasn't prepared for what he would look like after that message was delivered. His face is swollen, almost beyond recognition. Eyes puffed up, not quite closed but ringed with dark blue and purple streaks of bruising. A cut slices diagonally across one cheek and is sutured with several stitches. His lower lip is split in two places and there's a dark bruise along his right jawline. His left lower arm is in a cast, and the fingers peeking out are swollen and purple.

"Jesus Christ," I mutter as I take it all in, completely aghast at what he looks like. Not that I care he was hurt, but it's just shocking to see someone that beat up.

JT looks at me through pained eyes, the whites of which are now red from what I assume are burst blood vessels. "I look that bad?" he asks, his voice lisping with what could potentially be a split and swollen tongue the way he sounds.

"What in the fuck happened to you?" I ask with mock disbelief, even though I know damn well what happened to him.

JT stands from the bed, the back of his hospital gown flopping open. He moves like a ninety-year-old man and winces with every movement. His hand reaches out, points over to a chair where his clothes lie, and says, "Just let me get dressed and get me out of here. I'll tell you all about it when you get me home."

I don't argue with him, but hand him his clothes, carefully watching as every grimace and flash of pain plays across his face, and relishing in it. I thought I might have an ounce of compassion in me for anyone who's clearly hurting that badly, but it's not there. Not when I'm filled with the knowledge of Sela's pain and misery caused by his hands. On the contrary, it makes me almost giddy with happiness knowing he's hurting right now.

The release process is smooth as all the paperwork had been done. It was advised he be admitted for observation, but he declined, and after the necessary waivers were completed, the only thing they were insisting on was he have a ride home either by cab or by friend or family member. He called me, which means he wants to discuss money now.

Sela and I had been talking about this for days, and the best way to approach JT with a buyout when he asks for the money. I hope to God I stick to the script we created, which we felt was the best way to "handle" JT, and that this goes as smoothly as I hope. But for now, I silently wait him out as a nurse pushes him out in a wheelchair. I get my car, pull it up to the front, and JT is loaded into the front seat. We don't say a word during the short drive to his house in Sausalito, and he's utterly silent when we walk into the house.

I follow JT into his den, an ostentatious room filled with expensive leather furniture, two seventy-inch TVs, and a surround-sound system that cost a small fortune. He bypasses the couch and heads to the mahogany bar against one wall. Pulling out a crystal decanter filled with amber liquid, he pours almost a full glass. Without looking at me, he asks, "Want one?"

"No, man," I say quietly, trying to lace my voice with concern. "But I would like to know what happened to you. Were you in an accident?"

JT's shoulders jerk as he barks out a laugh, and then groans from the pain that movement caused. He takes a hefty swallow and hisses through his teeth after it goes down.

"You shouldn't drink if you're taking pain meds," I say, not out of any concern for him but because I want him lucid.

"I didn't take any pain meds," he grunts, and takes another slug. "I need a clear head."

Well, that makes two of us who need that.

"So what happened?" I prompt as he turns from the bar and walks over to one of the big couches that flank a large fireplace. The leather is buttery and the cushions are deep. He sinks into it slowly with a groan.

JT takes another sip, swallows it, and raises his bloodred eyes to me. "I'm in trouble."

So much trouble, I mentally agree. But I just raise my eyebrows in friendly worry.

"I got in deep with a bookie in Vegas. His enforcers paid me a visit this morning. That's why I look and feel like shit."

Here was part of what I had rehearsed with Sela. The need to be shocked by JT's revelation he could be in so deep. So I downplay any danger off the bat. "Well, what the fuck JT," I say with exasperation. "Pay the damn money. It's not like you don't have it."

"I don't," he says, takes another sip of bourbon. I can tell it's working on him because he starts to relax his body into the couch. "Have the type of money they're collecting, that is."

"What type of money are we talking about?" I ask hesitantly . . . my eyes wide with curiosity.

"Four million," he spits out, as if he can feel the bitterness of his debt on his tongue.

"Jesus fucking Christ," I explode, my jaw hanging wide at him in disbelief. "You've got to be fucking kidding me, JT, right?"

And the Oscar for this year's performance goes to . . . Beck North.

JT shakes his head and grimaces. "I wish I was kidding."

"What in the hell could you have bet four million dollars on?" I ask incredulously.

"The Mariota-VanZant fight."

Here I don't act surprised. JT knows me well enough to know I follow most all sports. He knows I'd know what that was. So I simply say, "You bet on VanZant."

"I was so sure he had what it takes," JT says in the frustrated voice of a gambler who just can't believe his luck has run out.

"Four million fucking dollars on a fucking fight, JT?" I grit out, letting a little bit of anger slip through. "Are you crazy to lay that type of money down on one fight?"

"It wasn't just one fight," he mutters.

"Explain," I demand. But I already know the story.

I made a bet . . . got two million in debt. Doubled down on Van-Zant. Figured it was a sure thing.

Yeah, that's what JT tells me, and I let me eyes flare wide in disbelief over his idiocy. Scrubbing my hand through my hair, I start pacing in front of him, acting the wigged-out, worried friend. "Well, pay the damn money. You owe it, pay it. It's better than getting the crap beat out of you."

"I don't have it," he whines, and I have to literally lock my legs to prevent myself from lunging at him. That "poor me" voice threatens to undo my resolve to lead JT along in my sinister plan.

"How can you not have it?" I ask in a measured voice.

He shrugs like a petulant child. "Come on, Beck. You know me. I'm irresponsible. I spend my money like it grows on trees. Anything solid is tied up in this house with no equity. The rest goes to fuel my expensive tastes. I could scrape up a million from some mutual funds; maybe two . . . but that's it, and it would take longer than what they've given me to liquidate. I'm tapped and strapped."

"How long do you have to pay it?" Because I'm dying to know what type of deadline they placed on him. That will tell me the date by which I'm hoping to have JT out of my life for good.

"Three days," he says, looking at me with pleading eyes. "I need you to loan it to me."

And here is where my real acting skills come in to play. Here is where I lay out the carefully scripted and rehearsed speech that truly doesn't take much acting at all if I let my real emotions come into play. And they do, because this fuckup is the biggest fuckup of his life, and JT knows my patience with him has been stretched thin over the past months with his poor choices and childish behavior.

I hold my hands up and take two steps back. "No way, JT. I am not bailing you out of this. I'm sure you can scrape up the money."

JT leans forward on the couch and winces while his knuckles turn white due to the death grip he has on his glass. "Beck . . . I'm telling you. I don't have it."

"Then get it from somewhere else," I snarl at him. "I'm not bailing your ass out. I've been telling you I'm sick of this shit, JT. You promised you were going on the straight and narrow and you lied to me."

"There's nowhere else for me to turn," JT says, and I swear I see a shimmer of tears in his eyes. "And Beck . . . they're not going to beat me up for the money. It's either a pay or don't type of situation."

"Meaning?" I ask with a tinge of fear in my voice for my "friend," whom I'm pissed as hell at but also appearing to still be worried about.

"They'll kill me. If they don't get their money, they'll kill me. Plain and simple."

"Goddamn," I shout out at the room as I spin away from him. Do another dramatic scrub of my hands through my hair. Turn to face JT, shoot him an accusatory look, and growl at him, "You goddamn motherfucking idiot, JT."

"I know," he says as he rises from the couch gingerly. He takes a step toward me. "I know, and I know I promised you I'd get things under control. But I was so sure this bet would get me out of trouble, and then I was going to shape my shit up. I promise this was the last stupid thing I'll do. I swear it."

I round on JT with fury etched all over my face. "I'm so sick of your lies, JT. Sick of living with this shadow over our business. You're a selfish asshole who cares for no one but yourself."

"I know, I know," he chants.

Taking in a deep breath, I lower my gaze and stare at the floor. I pretend to ponder his situation. I appear to be conflicted. Not once do I let go of the anger on my face so he never forgets that this is the most monumental fuckup he's made in our business and personal relationship.

Letting the air out of my lungs slowly, I take a step toward him, lean my head closer, and in a very soft but deadly serious voice, I tell him, "I'll give you the money—"

"Oh, man . . . thank you so much," he cuts in, but I hold my hand up. His mouth snaps shut.

"I'll give you the money, but it's not a loan and it's not a gift."

"What do you mean?" he asks carefully, and I notice his hand holding the half-empty tumbler of bourbon is shaking.

"It means I'll give you the four million, but consider it a buy-out from The Sugar Bowl. I want you out. I'm done with you."

JT's skin pales and his eyes go wide in disbelief. "No," he whispers.

"Yes," I maintain through gritted teeth. "I want you out of

my life, JT. You're nothing but a cancer to me. The four million will save your hide and compensate you for your share of the business."

"Like fuck it will," he spits out, his face now coloring red. "It's worth way more than that."

"Yeah, on paper it is. But it seems to me there's value in me giving you money that will help save you from getting killed. I'd say The Sugar Bowl in return for that is more than fair compensation for your life, right?"

"Beck . . . please . . . don't kick me out," he implores. "I don't have anything else."

"Not my fucking problem," I say softly. "But I tell you what . . . because The Sugar Bowl *is* worth more, I'll make it five million. Pay off your debt, and if you're wise, that extra million will keep you in style until you can figure out your next great adventure. Just know it's not going to be with me at your side."

JT doesn't respond, but just stares at me with wide, blinking eyes. His gaze is filled with pain, confusion, and even a little anger. But mostly, he looks lost. And this is what Sela and I had hoped for. That he wouldn't be able to reason out any better way out of this ordeal.

Fishing to my pocket, I pull out my car key and turn from JT. I don't even spare him a backward glance but tell him in no uncertain terms. "If you want the money to make your three-day deadline, you need to let me know sooner rather than later. I'll need at least a day to move some funds around."

"Beck," JT calls out to my retreating back, but I don't hesitate. I don't pause. I don't look at him again.

The offer's been made.

Now I just have to wait for him to pounce on it.

CHAPTER 21

. . . .

Sela

I step out onto Mission Street, leaving the glass-and-stone build-ing with redbrick walkways of Golden Gate University behind. The Millennium sits only two blocks away, but the bluish tint of the glass structure looks dull and faded as it reflects an overcast San Francisco day. There's a light mist falling, but it's relatively mild outside. Still, I pull my jacket collar up and quicken my pace toward our condo before it starts raining any harder.

Hitching my backpack up higher on my shoulder, I pull it around to my front so I can grab my cell phone out of the outer pocket. I turn it on as I make my way home, wanting to see if Beck has left me an update while I was in class today. He went into the office this morning to handle a few things, then he was meeting with his attorney to draft a buyout agreement for JT to sign.

If JT agreed to it, that is.

When Beck left him yesterday at his house, he was broken, alone, and pondering how his world was crashing down. Beck and I, on the other hand, were considering what a crapshoot this whole endeavor was. Would JT take the five million offered? Or would he try to figure some other way out of this mess just so he could keep his foot in the door at The Sugar Bowl?

My phone boots up and I don't see any new text messages awaiting, but there is a notification of a voice mail. Tapping the screen to pull it up, I peer at the phone number of whoever left the message. It's one I don't recognize, but figure maybe it's Beck calling from his attorney's office. Touching the Play icon, I put the phone to my ear and listen.

"Sela . . . it's JT. Can you please give me a call? It's important."

I'm stunned he's called me, and when I pull the phone back, I note he left the voice mail only about twenty minutes ago.

I don't call him back right away, instead using the short walk to the condo to try to figure out what in the hell he could possibly want from me. JT knows I don't like him. He knows I think he's a misogynist asshole. He, in turn, doesn't like me because I'm a threat to his relationship with Beck.

The doorman at the Millennium greets me by name and I give a return smile. I stare thoughtfully at my phone during the elevator ride up. Once inside, I dump my backpack on the couch and walk to our bedroom as I call JT.

He answers on the second ring. "Thanks for calling me back so quickly, Sela."

His voice is pleasant and polite, two things I bet he's struggling with mightily right now. "I was in class," I tell him. "My phone was turned off."

"Right," he says, although I'm sure the fact I'm a student means nothing to him. He only sees me as a Sugar Baby. "So, I was wanting to talk to you about Beck and The Sugar Bowl."

"What about it?" I ask vaguely, playing dumb as best I can.

"I know he told you about his offer to me last night to buy me out, right?"

I could lie to JT and deny it, but he wouldn't buy it. I can tell by the tone of his voice, and the mere fact he's reached out to me that he knows in his heart of hearts that Beck and I are solid. No matter what bull Beck may have been feeding him last week about putting the brakes on, JT calling me makes it clear he thinks I hold influence.

And . . . if I can help this deal get pushed through, then even better.

"Yeah . . . he told me you needed some money and that he'll give it to you in exchange for transfer of your ownership interest," I admit to him.

"It's not a good deal for me," JT says adamantly. "But I think I have a better solution for all of us. It will give us both what we want."

"What's that?" I ask, now intrigued about what scheme he's cooked up.

"I'd like to sit down and discuss this with you in person. Go over my idea, which is a little complex. I want you to tell me what you think, and whether you think Beck would be receptive to it. I don't have a lot of time, given the deadline by which I need the money, so I was hoping we could meet now."

I am free the rest of the day, but I'm not sure I should get involved. Beck laid down the ultimatum. It's up to JT to take it or turn it down. But then the part of me that worries that JT will make things messy for Beck and The Sugar Bowl feels compelled to hear him out. Perhaps help to talk some sense into him. Make him see the benefit of taking the money and getting out. Help to convince him that Beck won't back down on this and there's no room to negotiate.

Of course, the one thing that I've truly got to consider is my hair color. I'd colored it back to as close to my natural state as I could get it, with the idea in mind I wouldn't be crossing paths with JT again. Will he recognize me now?

My gut says he won't. That he's such a self-absorbed person that he wouldn't recognize my face. He's seen it plenty of times, no matter my hair color, and he hasn't shown the slightest bit of recollection.

It would be a risk, no doubt. It could compromise everything.

But I could help to put the nail in his coffin if I can convince him it's a fool's errand to try to get more out of Beck than what he's offered to him. Make him understand that he's in a precarious position and that it's well worth the trade-off . . . The Sugar Bowl for his life.

I laugh inside. Little does he know that he may walk away with his life intact, but if I have anything to do with it, he'll be sitting behind bars with that precious life of his.

"I could meet you somewhere," I say, throwing caution to the wind.

JT gives a mirthless laugh into the phone. "Um . . . yeah . . . not sure how much Beck told you about my condition, but I can barely get off the couch. Can you come here . . . to my house?"

I look around the bedroom, taking in the pale blue walls, teak colored furniture, and pristine white bedding. It's my favorite place in the condo because it's so peaceful and relaxing. This is my life now, with Beck, and I'll do whatever needs to be done to ensure I maintain it.

Walking over to the nightstand on my side of the bed, I open the drawer. "Text me your address. I can be there in less than an hour."

"Will do. And thank you, Sela," JT says, sounding immensely grateful to me.

I disconnect, wondering what he has up his sleeve. I don't trust his polite but pitiful demeanor. He's absolutely lying when he says he has a plan that would benefit both him and Beck.

Doesn't mean he doesn't have some sort of plan he wants to run by me, but I guarantee you it's all to his benefit alone.

Which is why I'm going to his house to meet with him. I need to know what he's up to so our plans don't get derailed.

Reaching into my drawer, I pull out my gun.

I'm not scared of JT, but I'm damn well making sure I'm protected in case he recognizes me and things go bad.

Walking into the closet, I grab a medium-size black satchel purse and stow the gun in there. I consider for just a crazy moment calling Beck and telling him what's going on, but then I immediately discount it just as quickly. He'll forbid me from going, and he'd be right to do so. I'd in turn get affronted by his attempts to control me and prevent me from helping. It will lead to an epic argument, with me not heeding his advice and heading to JT's house anyway. That would also lead to Beck leaving his attorney's office and trying to cut me off at JT's house. It would be an ugly scene, so I choose not to tell Beck what is going on.

But I do want to call someone else and fill them in on some of the details of what's been going on in my life.

Someone who deserves to know what's happening.

I use the bathroom and wash my hands. Then I transfer my wallet and keys from my backpack to the black purse and head to the parking garage. This will be only the third time I've driven my new car from Beck. There's no need living here in the city, but we did go out on Christmas day for a little drive to Half Moon Bay, and then again yesterday we drove it to my apartment in Oakland, where I gathered the last of my possessions I had stored there, and closed that door on my life for good.

After I get into the car and pull out of the parking garage, I depress the phone button on the steering wheel. This pairs my phone with the Bluetooth and offers me voice activation.

"Call Dad's cell phone," I say.

A woman's voice, cultured and polished, says, "Calling Dad's cell phone."

A few clicks and then it's ringing. He answers like only a father should. "What's up, baby girl?"

I smile. He's my dad, he's great, and I love him.

But I haven't been fair to him either.

"Hey . . . you got a few minutes to talk?" I ask softly, feeling slightly weird by talking to him through the car's speakers.

"Always for you. What's up?"

"I need to tell you something," I say carefully, trying to keep a lighthearted tone. "It's going to throw you for a loop, but I need you to listen and then you can berate me for keeping it from you and give me sage advice."

"You didn't run off and join the circus did you?" he quips.

I want to laugh, but he's not going to be laughing in just a few minutes, so I tell him straight by cutting to the chase. "I've identified one of them."

I can literally hear my father release a long, pained breath, because he knows exactly what I'm talking about. "You did?"

"About nine months ago . . . I saw him on TV and recognized the red bird tattoo."

My father knows about the tattoo. He and my mother sat with me, each holding a hand as I recounted to the police as best I could the spotty details of what I remembered.

"Jesus, Sela," he says in astonishment. "Why didn't you go to the police? We need to go to the police."

"I am," I assure him. "Soon . . . probably this week. But I need to tell you some stuff about him that you're not going to like. Some stuff that I was planning on doing that you're really not going to like."

"You can tell me anything," he reassures me, which I already know. It makes me ashamed that he wasn't the first person I told on that horrid day long ago when I saw JT on the television.

Taking a deep breath, I tell him as succinctly as I can just the crucial details. "It's JT . . . I mean Jonathon Townsend, Beck's partner."

Dad curses, but I talk over him, needing to get it all out. "When I realized who he was, I considered going to the police, but then quickly discounted it. I was afraid they couldn't do anything because of the memory issues, but more important, I wanted JT to suffer for what he did. I also wanted to know who the other men were that night. So my plan was to confront JT with a gun, force him to tell me what I needed to know, and then I was going to kill him."

"Are you kidding me?" my dad yells into the phone.

"Dad . . . I didn't go through with that plan," I say quickly in an effort to keep him focused.

"But you were going to kill him?" my dad asks, sounding incredulous. "Do you know how insane that is?"

"Yes, I get that," I assure him. "I was driven by a lot of hate and anger and was acting rashly, but I've got that under control now. That night I went to confront JT . . . well, I met Beck instead."

"Does he know?" dad asks quietly.

"Yes, he does. And we're currently working on a plan to get JT out of The Sugar Bowl first before we go to the police. Get things cleaned up on Beck's end so that hopefully when JT's arrested, it won't affect the business."

"It will still blow back on Beck," my dad says.

And that's true. When this hits the media, it's going to be about how the former co-owner of The Sugar Bowl is charged with rape. Beck's business will take a hit. "We know, but it's still going to be much easier to have JT removed as owner. If he still owns part of The Sugar Bowl when he's arrested, Beck will have to run things by him, and you know that will be a nightmare. Hell, JT's going to be so mad he'll fight against Beck on everything . . . probably will try to intentionally run it into the ground. It will be tough on everyone once this goes public, but we'll get through it."

"Of course we'll get through it," he says soothingly. "I'm right there by your side."

"The police may not think my identification of him by that tattoo is strong enough to force him to give DNA," I tell my dad. "He may stay free."

"And if that happens, what's your plan then?" my dad asks hesitantly. And I know what he's thinking . . . will I revert back to my original plan for murder?

"Then I'll have to live my life content to know that while I might not get justice for what happened to me, that I got Beck instead. And trust me . . . that will be enough."

I think.

God, I hope.

I really, really hope I can let it go if it comes to that.

. . . .

CHAPTER 22

Beck

I open the door to Michael Mina, an upscale, elegant San Francisco restaurant. Due to the abundant natural light from large windows in both the front and back of the restaurant, I easily spot Dennis sitting in a booth about midway back. He raises a hand in greeting and pointing to him, I tell the hostess, "I'm meeting someone and I see him over there."

She smiles and gives me a polite nod, murmuring, "Enjoy your meal."

He doesn't bother standing in professional acknowledgment of me, and I like that. After watching the fight with him the other night, and hell, after all the personal shit he knows about Sela and me, I much prefer to think of him as just a friend in this moment.

Because that's exactly what I need right now.

I had called Dennis a few hours ago when I got to my attorney's office and asked if he had time to meet today. He invited me to lunch, even boasting he'd pay for it, since he'd finally cashed the check I'd given him.

"What's up?" he says casually as I slide into the seat opposite him.

"Just finished a meeting with my attorney. He's drafting up a purchase agreement for JT to sign if he takes the five-million-dollar offer. Should be ready in a few hours."

"Think he will?" Dennis asks. I had called him yesterday evening and told him briefly about JT's ass kicking. He didn't seem all that surprised it happened so quickly after the fight, stating that the timing of it was a good way to deliver the message of what a dire situation JT had put himself in and that his bookie was not fucking around on collecting.

Shrugging, I reach out and take a slice of bread from the basket that sits between us. "No clue. Not only was he rattled from the beating, but I caught him off guard by using his situation as leverage to get him out of the company. I figure he's reeling right now, and it's hard to make good decisions like that."

"Well, hopefully the fear of what will happen to him if he doesn't come up with the money will motivate him to see things your way."

"Hopefully," I agree, my mind not really focusing on that. I've realized that I have no further control over this situation and our next move depends solely on what JT decides to do.

A waiter approaches our table and sets a glass of ice water in front of me before rattling off the lunch specials. I've eaten here several times and it's always been good, I ask him to just bring me whatever he thinks is best. Dennis orders the Prime Black Angus rib eye rare with a loaded potato. We both stick with water for our drinks.

"I'm flying out tonight to Vegas," Dennis says after the waiter leaves. "VanZant's still there and I'm going to deliver the money."

"Not using the middle man?"

"He's good and trustworthy," Dennis says with a dark laugh, "but there's no one I trust enough when that amount of cash is involved."

I don't ask how it's being delivered or the details. Dennis has warned Sela and me enough that we don't need the details of how he operates, and we're safer not knowing. I have to trust he knows what he's doing and stop worrying about details I have no control over. And frankly, I just don't want to know how Dennis managed to "launder" the money I gave him into what is now probably five hundred thousand in nonsequential bills filling a sturdy briefcase.

I nod in understanding, but don't respond. I'm too keyed up over what's happened in the last two days, too worried about everything that could still be screwed up. I'm trying to make contingency plans, and it's like playing a game of chess with an opponent who flies by the seat of his pants.

"VanZant's an interesting character," Dennis says, and my eyes dart to his.

"How so?" I ask, not really caring, because let's face it . . . I'm done with him. But I've also learned enough about Dennis to know he always has a point to everything.

"From a small town in Iowa, captain of the wrestling squad. Honors student who dated the homecoming queen. Full scholarship to Purdue. Just a golden boy."

I break off a piece of bread, pop it into my mouth, and wait for Dennis to make his point.

"Just one of those guys you knew was going to be a success in life," he says as he leans his forearms on the table. "Got married to his sweetheart after college, produced two cute kids, and found out he had an actual talent for mixed martial arts."

While I know Dennis is leading me somewhere, I'm antsy with my own worries, so I urge him along. "Sounds like he's a little slice of Americana, but so what?"

"He didn't bat an eye at accepting a bribe," Dennis says. "On paper . . . just looking at him from the outside . . . you'd never think that boy would do something like that. Too much straight and narrow in him. But he took it all the same."

"Meaning?" I prompt.

"Meaning that everyone has a price and everything can be bought if you know the right people, so with that in mind, I'm going to push you right along and ask you to spill it. What do you want from me?"

Perceptive fuck. But then again, that's why I paid him big bucks so far, and why I'm getting ready to have a conversation that could damn me to hell.

I like Dennis Flaherty a lot. He's not only a competent professional who came personally and highly recommended, but he's proven to me that he can get the job done. On top of that, I just think he's an upstanding guy. He clearly has shady ties, but you can tell that he's motivated to do good by others.

Most important, he also understands vengeance and how there can be an unquenchable need for it when someone you care for has been hurt.

Placing the bread on a small plate, I pick up my water, take a sip, and then set it down. Looking him square in the eye, I come right to the point. "I need a backup plan if everything we're hoping to happen goes to shit. If I can't get JT out of The Sugar Bowl. If the police don't believe Sela's memory is enough to investigate. Sela and I have talked about just walking away from it all, but I don't think I can fucking do that. I need another plan."

"A plan to keep The Sugar Bowl or a plan to get justice?" Dennis asks calmly. "Because those are two very different goals."

"I don't care about The Sugar Bowl. I'm talking about JT."

"Everyone has a price and everything can be bought," Dennis says, repeating his words from just moments ago. "What do you want to buy?"

I figure if I'm man enough to want this to happen, I can be man enough to tell Dennis what I want without hesitation. "JT's death."

Dennis doesn't react. No cough of surprise, no raised eyebrows. He just nods in understanding. "I've got the necessary resources to make that happen."

"I don't want you—" I say hastily, because I don't want him at risk.

Dennis holds up a quick hand to stop me. "Not me. But I can facilitate what you need with the right people who will do it cleanly and without any suspicion."

The minute those words hit my ears, I feel a sudden weight fall from my shoulders, even if a ball of black disgust with myself starts to form deep in my stomach. I can't let Sela go unavenged. While I'd like JT to pay for his crimes within the bounds of the law, I'm prepared to take action so Sela won't be failed again.

"Good," I whisper, looking down at my hands. Am I really asking this man to facilitate murder for me? I think back to how shocked I was when Sela first told me she wanted to kill JT. I thought it was an insane proposition and that the risk of getting caught was too great to bear.

And yet here I am . . . trying to figure out how to make it happen.

"But doing it without raising suspicion means more than just how and where it's carried out," Dennis explains with an ominous undertone. "The police always look to those closest to the victim. That means family, close friends, and business partners. What's been the nature of your relationship with JT over the last several months?"

"You mean, how we get along?"

"Exactly. If the police were to go to your staff members, are they going to say that you are a solid duo who has each other's backs? That you care for and respect one another, and that in a million years they could never imagine you harming JT?"

I swallow hard, because, no . . . they wouldn't say that at all. While Linda would never want to hurt me or get me in trouble, she's as honest as the day is long. She'll have to tell them she's seen my frustrations with JT's behavior. The endless list of women complaining about him and my actions in smoothing things over to keep the business strong. JT's secretary, Karla, who *is* loyal to her boss and doesn't care for me because I treat my employees well and she gets treated like shit, will relish in telling them about the fights we've had in JT's office. I guarantee she's listened in on them, certain that on more than one occasion she's heard me telling JT I want to buy him out and him refusing. She's aware of JT's bad behavior as well, and has seen my fury over it time and again. I bet she'd go so far as to say that she's seen murder in my eyes when I've stalked into JT's office before, and she wouldn't be wrong. Of course, back then, it was metaphorical murder, but really . . . how hard would that be for the police to leap to actual murder?

Add that to the fact that my girlfriend was raped by JT, and they'll have enough circumstantial evidence to come after me for the crime. My attorney would never disclose any communications we've had, as they're protected by attorney-client privilege. But that doesn't mean JT's attorney won't also confirm that I've made overtures to buy JT out, and that JT's own attorney has advised him there's no need to entertain offers because of the way it's written.

The argument will be simple enough. I wanted JT out of The Sugar Bowl because he was a liability. He refused. JT raped my girlfriend. I exacted vengeance and removed him from my business all in one fell swoop.

Yeah . . . the police would look directly to me.

"I'd be a prime suspect," I tell Dennis, and then tell him exactly how strained our relationship has been for several months.

"Then we'd have to try to direct attention and evidence to a better suspect," Dennis says simply.

"His bookie?" I guess.

"His bookie, the Sugar Babies he's tried to harm or has harmed, people he's bought drugs from. JT's into some whacked shit. It will help to muddy the waters of the suspect list."

"How would the police even know about his betting?" I ask. I know virtually nothing about this type of stuff.

"JT's talked to Vegas on the phone, so there will be a record of that. And his bookie is well known. They won't have a hard time connecting those dots. And frankly, if JT doesn't take your money and chooses to risk his own life, there's a good chance Vegas will take care of the problem for you."

"If only I could be so lucky," I mutter as I look around the restaurant. "But there's a chance they won't kill him too, right? I mean . . . what if he hands them a few million he can scrape up and works out a payment plan? He makes a good enough salary that if he stopped spending his money so frivolously, he could get them paid off other ways."

"That could happen too," Dennis agrees. "You gotta figure those people who take bets are businessmen too. They could extend part of the repayment and call it a loan. Attach a ridiculous amount of interest to it. They're in the business of making fast money and look at return on investment too. His bookie could go to loan shark pretty quickly."

"Fuck," I grit out. "I hate this shit. Hate seeing justice for Sela and happiness for us both just within our reach and about a million fucking things that could go wrong. It's driving me crazy."

"Look, man," Dennis says, and his voice is so empathetic it gives me pause. "You know I understand how you're feeling right now. I've been in your shoes, and there was nothing that was going to stop me from avenging Rosa. I had her father and brothers behind me, but I'm the one who sleeps the best at night for ending the fuck who took her from us. No one will understand what you're going through better than me. But with that being said, you've got a lot more to lose that I ever did. My love was what I had lost. Yours is still very much alive and the biggest part of your happiness. Shit goes down in a bad way and you get caught for this, you're going to lose something that's far more important than what little bit of peace you'll get from ending JT."

And he's nailed the dilemma. Balancing pros and cons, trying to figure out what my priorities are and where I need to be focusing my attention. Avenging Sela and ridding this world of JT, or living happily ever after with a kernel of regret for letting him go free. Those are my choices and they are not easy ones to make.

"Regardless of what you decide," Dennis continues in a low voice, "you've got to let some time pass before you move on it. You've got to start publicly repairing your relationship with him, and get some distance between you and the tension you two have exhibited to others over the past months. It might mean you need to continue working side by side with him for months to make sure you are shown in the best possible light. Think you could honestly do that?"

"No," I say immediately. "I can't be around him. If JT stays in The Sugar Bowl, I'm going to need to walk. I can't live that type of lie."

"Then my advice is still the same," he says. "Let JT buy you out. Make it amicable. Part on good terms. Then you walk and don't look back. When some time has passed, and if you still need vengeance, then we'll talk some more and I'll get you set up."

After the waiter brings out our meals, which look delicious, and leaves, I ask Dennis, "So what's up for you after your trip to Vegas?"

"I've actually got a wedding to attend in Ireland this weekend, so I'll fly out from Vegas to New York, and from there into Shannon. My cousin's getting married and I will take any excuse to get back to the motherland. While I'm not a big fan of weddings in general, Irish ones are a hell of a lot of fun."

"Yeah . . . red hair, fair skin, tough-as-nails attitude, and boyish charm. I kind of pegged you as Irish," I say with a smirk as I cut into a huge scallop. "But I don't detect an accent."

"I was born in New York, but both my parents are from Ballinderreen, a little village in County Galway. They're Irish folk musicians and emigrated to the Big Apple to see if they could find their fame and fortune there."

"And did they?"

"No more than what they found playing in the local pubs back home," Dennis says with a laugh. "But they liked the opportunities, especially for their kids, so they stayed."

"You go to Ireland a lot?" I ask.

"I do," he says while lifting a bite of steak to his mouth. "And I don't have any major projects on tap, so I'm going to stay there for a few days, then I have a guys' trip planned to do some deepsea fishing down in Panama. Wanna come?"

"Who are the 'guys'?" I ask.

"People who could potentially help you down the road one day," he says with a knowing smile.

"I think I'll pass," I say with a chuckle. "You told me to be all straight and narrow in case I need help with JT down the road. I don't think a trip on the books with your boys would look good."

"That's true," he says as he cuts another bite of steak. "Maybe one day . . . after all this shit's done."

"One day," I agree.

We enjoy our meal and discuss other things that don't revolve around bribes and murder. We talk like friends, and this I like a lot. There's no doubt that once this period of my life starts receding into the distance, Dennis Flaherty will remain a friend to me and Sela. I hope Dennis can find love again, because he deserves to have what I've found.

The day is half over and it's been productive so far. I have my attorney working on the necessary paperwork to get JT out of my business. Dennis is taking care of the payoff to VanZant. And this evening, Caroline and Ally are coming to dinner. Actually, I'm going to take Ally out to dinner and Caroline and Sela are going to talk over wine and cheese. Or maybe pizza and beer, who knows.

This was Sela's idea. She wants Caroline to know what happened to her and that she now has someone she can talk to about it. Someone who understands the pain, humiliation, and self-hatred. I have no idea how much Sela will tell her. She's not sure herself and said she'd play it by ear, but whatever she chooses to reveal, I'm sure it will be exactly the right amount. Caroline is someone I trust with my life, and Sela knows her secrets and can be trusted with her as well.

And then all that's left to do is to wait and see what JT decides to do.

CHAPTER 23

. . . .

Sela

Beck calls me again and I let it ring through to voice mail. He called about ten minutes ago and I didn't answer, knowing he would hear the tension in my voice. Knowing that I wouldn't be able to lie to him when he asked where I was. I listened to his first voice mail, my heart twinging with guilt that I'm avoiding him, but I know he'd go crazy if he knew I was sitting in JT's driveway right now.

I have no business being here. It's stupid and illogical, but I can't fucking help myself. Maybe I need to stand in his presence one more time before he goes down, or maybe I feel like I could help urge him along to make the right decision. Whatever the insanity of my reason, here I am and here I will remain until I hear what he has to say.

Beck's first voice mail to me was simple and sweet.

"Hey babe . . . just finished lunch with Dennis and on my way home. Wanted to know if you needed anything while I was out. Call me if you do, otherwise see you in about fifteen, twenty minutes."

That was half an hour ago, and I would bet my last dollar that the voice mail he just left is wondering where the hell I am. I'm sure he's at the condo now, flummoxed that I'm not there when I should be and didn't leave a note as to when I'd be back. Not that he keeps track of me or anything, but it's just a common courtesy we've offered each other since we started living together. If I'm going out, I'll leave him a note. He does the same for me.

I didn't do it this time, not because I was afraid of the lie, but merely because I was so distracted with thoughts of JT and what he could possibly want to talk to me about, I just didn't think about it as I left the condo and locked up behind me.

But that's done and Beck is just going to have to wait for me to come home tonight and tell him what I've been doing. He's going to go nuts, and I expect it will lead to a massively huge fight. This is unfortunate, because Caroline's coming over to talk, and it's going to suck if Beck's pissed at me, but oh well. He'll get over it eventually.

JT's home is beautiful, but I expected no less given his spending habits. It's three levels done in a dark gray plank siding with brown trim. The driveway is paved in cobblestone and curves past a raised garden bed filled with bushes and small flowering trees that provide privacy. I can glimpse the bay between his house and the one next to it.

Sucking in a lungful of oxygen, I turn the car off and exhale slowly before exiting. I grab my purse, hitch it over my shoulder, and nervously tuck my hair behind my ears. My pulse is thundering, not at the prospect of seeing JT, but of him possibly recognizing me, and I suppose that will happen within the first few moments of him seeing me.

I step onto the front porch, but before I can even raise my hand to ring the bell, the massive carved wooden door opens and I'm standing face-to-face with JT. Although Beck described his appearance to me, I'm still shocked by his appearance. Deep purple with tinges of green covers most of his face, and his jaw is swollen and bruised. A cut is sutured on one cheek and his lower lip is scabbed. His left arm is in a cast, which he gingerly supports against his ribs.

I take all of this in even as I watch JT examining my new hair color. His eyebrows raise a tad in surprise, but otherwise he doesn't seem to recognize the girl he once raped all those years ago. In fact, he doesn't comment about my appearance and merely steps back while motioning me inside.

"Thanks for coming," he says by way of greeting, but it sounds hollow and wooden.

I step into his house, which immediately opens up into a great room that overlooks the bay with peaked ceilings and large windows. The floors are covered in blond wood polished to a high sheen. His furniture is contemporary, done in silver, mauve, and black with chrome accents.

JT turns his back on me and veers off a short hall to the right. "Let's go back in my den. The furniture's more comfortable in there."

Clutching my purse a bit tighter to me, I follow JT. He moves slowly and there's no doubt he's in pain from his beating. Even as nervous as I am to be here, seeing him like this brings me a small measure of joy.

He enters another large room that sits at the back of the house, also with large windows to take in the beauty of the bay and the San Francisco skyline, but here the furniture is a bit more transitional and definitely more comfortable looking. JT's clearly been spending time on the sumptuous-looking couch because there's a pillow and a blanket lying there.

As I take in my surroundings, JT walks over to a bar and pours himself a glass of what appears to be bourbon. He doesn't look at me but asks, "Want something to drink?"

"I'm good," I say, pleased that my voice sounds strong and

calm, even as my heart is thumping hard over being in such close proximity to him. "So what did you want to talk to me about?"

JT tilts the glass back, slugs down the liquor he just poured, and pours another two fingers. When he turns back to look at me, he merely leans back against the bar and says, "Did Beck tell you everything?"

There's no sense in lying, but no need for details either. "Just that you lost a bet and needed money fast. Judging by the look of you, I'm guessing that's true."

JT grimaces and nods, cutting right to the chase. His voice is bitter when he says, "I can't give up The Sugar Bowl, Sela. It's all I have. I called Beck's dad last night and asked him for the money, but he declined. I'm out of options and you're sort of my last resort. I'm hoping you could talk to Beck on my behalf."

This is interesting news . . . that JT went to Mr. North. Even more relieving that he kept his word and turned down JT.

JT looks at me with hopeful eyes and I find it utterly ironic that he's coming to me for help. I try to keep my tone neutral when I say, "Beck's mind seemed made up. I'm not sure what I could do."

"Oh, cut the shit," JT growls as he stands straighter. Waving the glass he holds in his good hand at me, causing some bourbon to slosh out, he says, "You hold a lot of power over Beck and don't pretend otherwise. But you are right . . . I think his mind is made up, but I bet you could sway him if you wanted, and I have a counterproposal that will interest him."

But I don't want to sway him, asshole. I want you to suffer.

"What could that possibly be?" I ask, because this is the real reason I'm here. I need to know what JT may have up his sleeve, and it has to be something if he thinks it will change Beck's mind.

JT downs the rest of the liquor and sets the glass on the bar behind him. When he turns back to me, his eyes are cold and calculating. "I'm prepared to renounce my inheritance rights to the North fortune. I've even had my attorney draft up a proposed agreement if Beck will loan me the money to get me out of my current jam and let me retain my rights in The Sugar Bowl."

I can't help the sudden gasp of surprise or the way my eyes open wide over JT's statement. It's a dead giveaway that Beck has indeed told me all there is to know.

JT gives a malicious laugh. "I can tell by the look on your face you know Beckett North, Sr., is my father too, but more important, you're stunned *I* know this information."

"But how?" I mutter. If Beck's dad is to be believed, he never told JT.

"My mother," JT says simply. "She told me years ago. Wanted me to know so I could claim what was rightfully mine one day."

Holy shit. He knows. He knows Beck is his brother, and by the looks of it, he's got his sights set on the North money.

"That won't change his mind," I whisper, because I know without a doubt it won't. Beck doesn't give a shit about his father's money.

"Bullshit," JT yells at me, his face turning red underneath the purple bruises. He takes a step toward me and snarls, "You could persuade him. You fucking hold his nuts in your greedy little hands."

I take a wary step back, clutching my purse tighter. JT's face is a mask of livid rage as he matches my movement. My pulse skitters away from me as I consider making a running break out of this house. "I think you need to discuss this with Beck. Maybe this will sway him, but I shouldn't be involved with this."

I take another step back but JT's words freeze me in place just by the sheer hatred in his tone as he rasps, "You fucking bitch.

This is all because of you. Beck changed the minute you walked into his life, and I frankly can't understand what in the hell he sees in a whore like you."

By all accounts, I should turn and get the hell away from this enraged man who had once hurt me so badly I didn't think I'd ever recover. But instead, anger swells up and I stand my ground with the knowledge I have a gun to protect me if needed. "You asshole," I sneer at him. "This is all on you. You made stupid decisions and now you need to man up and accept the consequences, you jackass."

It's almost as if a pool of red-hot fury fills JT's eyes and his jaw tightens so hard I'm expecting him to crack teeth. I think for a moment he might tell me to get out of his house, but instead he starts to walk toward me in almost a zombielike fashion, his right hand curled into a tight fist as his chest rises and falls sharply. I know without a doubt he's overwhelmed with rage at the situation and with me, and he intends to lash out . . . probably physically. Before he can reach me though, my hand dips into my purse and I pull out my gun, holding it aimed directly at his heart.

He stops in midstride and his eyes slowly slide to the gun. I expect him to be cowed, but instead when he looks back at me his lips curl upward and he taunts, "Going to shoot me, Sela?"

"You take another step closer, and I will," I tell him with a quavering voice. "Now I'm going to leave—"

"You won't do it," he says softly, talking right over me. His voice so assured, he starts moving toward me again. Deliberate steps without a stutter of caution in them.

Almost a cocky swagger.

He looks utterly deranged and my hand starts shaking as my finger tightens on the trigger.

"I dare you," JT whispers, and then gives a husky laugh. "I dare you to fucking do it, Sela."

My hand shakes harder and he's only two steps away from me.

"Go on," he urges me softly, putting one foot in front of the other. "You know you want to."

Tears sting at my eyes because the urge to pull the trigger is so intense, and yet my moral conscience isn't letting me do it. It's not letting me fucking avenge myself nor protect myself.

JT takes the last step and he walks right into the gun until the barrel is pressed into his chest. He laughs at me and says ever so softly, "Can't do it, can you?"

I don't admit defeat though, and bring my other hand up to steady the gun. "If you don't—"

JT moves so suddenly I can't react. His casted arm swings hard, catching me at my wrist and causing my gun to go flying, where it clatters across the hardwood floors. JT's good hand—and I find out quickly enough it's his dominant hand because it's brutally strong—wraps around the front of my throat.

"You goddamn filthy cunt," he screams at me, spit flying from his mouth and spattering on my face. With his hand clamped tightly on my throat, he marches me backward across the floor. "Think you can come into my life and fuck with what's mine?"

My butt slams into something and I vaguely recall a large desk sitting catercorner. Although my momentum is stopped, JT's isn't and he pushes me right onto the desk with his hand on my throat. He leans his entire body weight into me . . . against me . . . and vomit rises in my throat that his body's touching mine.

I bend backward until my spine hits the desk, JT coming to lay on top of me. For added leverage, he places his casted arm across my chest. Scenes from my rape flash before me, except now I can see JT's face in my memory as clear as day. Now that I know who he is, I can see his ugly face twisted in sickening pleasure as he pumps away on top of me. Both my hands come up to latch on to his wrist in a desperate attempt to dislodge his grip. My legs start kicking furiously, trying to get purchase on the hardwood floor, but just the tips of my sneakers can touch and won't grab hold to give me leverage.

As he leans in toward me, JT's face twists into an ugly grimace and the reeking fumes of alcohol wash across my face. "You're still a mess, Sela."

Those words . . .

You're a mess.

Still a mess . . .

My eyes go round with understanding and JT nods vigorously at me, his cracked lips peeling back, stretching so tight in a macabre smile that they start to ooze blood. "That's right, Sela. Did you think the brown hair would throw me off? Think I wouldn't recognize that face . . . that mouth . . . that throat that swallowed my cum? One of the best fucks I've ever had and you didn't think I wouldn't remember that?"

I go dizzy at the implication, my lungs deflating with the realization that JT knows who I am.

He. Knows. Who. I. Am.

"I didn't see it right away," JT whispers, his face hovering just over mine. "Not that night at the mixer. But in Beck's office . . . in the clear light of day, and frankly, I was sober then . . . I saw it. Knew exactly who you were, and I had to wonder why in the fuck you'd bother to come back into my life."

"You sick fuck," I scream at him, trying to buck but having no leverage. "Get off me."

JT's hand tightens on my throat, his cast pushing harder on my chest. My lungs compress and I fight to drag in a tiny breath of precious oxygen.

"I have to assume you told Beck all about our interlude at that party, right?" JT taunts. "Otherwise, why would he be so determined to get me out of The Sugar Bowl?"

I try to shake my head in the negative, feed him a lie so that perhaps he doesn't see me as a threat, but he merely responds by gripping me harder.

"I have to admit," he says, eyes wild with fevered craze. "You're in a very tempting position. I could fuck you raw right now and not a damn thing you could do about it."

"Get off," I wheeze, my vision starting to go blurry.

He ignores me, shifts his weight. For a brief and blessed moment, his hand relaxes and I drag in air that feels like razors against my bruised neck. But he merely moves his casted arm upward and places it at the base my throat and presses down. My hands release his wrist and move to the cast, trying to push him off. "But I don't have time for that. I've got bigger problems . . . namely that you're a major threat to my existence. Why you haven't gone to the cops yet is beyond me, but fuck if I'll take that chance now."

He leans his weight on me. A gray haze starts to crowd my peripheral vision and an image of Beck's face flashes before me.

"One more thing I want you to know before I end you," JT says in a soft voice . . . almost lovingly. "Surely you know you're not my first, and definitely weren't my last. In these next few moments, when I'm choking the life out of you, I want you to go with the knowledge that you're not the only girl of Beck's who caught my attention. Sweet Caroline was a lovely piece that I just couldn't resist, and she put up a much bigger fight than you ever did, which made it all the better for me."

My eyes flare wide and a surge of anger pulses through me as I understand what he's saying.

God . . . JT raped Caroline? He's Ally's father?

"That's right," he says with a laugh as he reads the expression on my face. "Slipped her a little Rohypnol in her drink at her parents' Christmas party, followed her home, and when her date dropped her off, she was easy pickings."

I growl against the weight of his cast on my throat, narrowing my eyes at him with hatred. As incomprehensible as it is, I have no choice but to believe him. I try to pull in air but get nothing. My hands release my hold on his cast, and I start to flail in a desperate attempt to do something. Find something to help me live through this, and avenge not only myself but Caroline as well.

But as the lack of oxygen starts to shut my body down, the gray gets darker, I feel myself starting to give in to the pull of oblivion.

CHAPTER 24

. . . .

Beck

I glance at the clock on the mantel for maybe the hundredth time, the nauseating feeling of unease that's been steadily increasing over the last hour threatening to expel the Michael Mina scallops. I pull my phone out of my pocket and dial Sela again. It rings only twice before going directly to voice mail, but I don't bother leaving another message. She'll get the point I'm worried when she listens to the other two I've left.

I have no clue where she is or why she hasn't responded to me, but this is what I do know. Her last class got out at one P.M., just about the time I was with Dennis. She had told me that morning she had planned to come back to the condo and do some studying here, and we knew that Caroline and Ally would be arriving roughly around four thirty or so, depending on the drive after Caroline got off work and picked Ally up from preschool. When I got home around two thirty, it was to an empty condo.

Fine. No problem. Maybe Sela decided to study at Golden Gate's library. She does that sometimes. Or maybe she went to the grocery store. Not out of the realm of possibility, although we tend to eat out more than we cook in.

Still, plausible possibilities and I know I shouldn't worry.

Except I am, because the one thing Sela wouldn't do is ignore my calls. She would have texted me her change of plans. And if she was unable to take my first call for some reason, she absolutely would have called me back once she got my first message, which was left almost two hours ago.

Something's wrong. I can feel it deep in my gut. It actually makes my bones ache.

Add on top of that, I haven't heard a peep from JT today, and my trouble radar is going haywire. He should have called by now, as he knows his deadline is looming. I had hoped for the call to come saying he accepted my offer. At the very least, I expected a call from him trying to get me to change my mind. I knew it was a distinct possibility JT wasn't going to just roll over and take what I offered. He's a businessman first and foremost. He would try to negotiate, of that I'm sure. He would try to find leverage over me, and he'd use it to his benefit.

And now Sela seems to be off the grid, and she would be the biggest source of leverage JT could get his hands on.

But no.

That's fucking ridiculous to even think that JT would have Sela. Or that Sela would go near JT. Or that she's anywhere other than the library studying, for some reason forgot to text me, and has her phone off so as not to disturb others.

The doorbell rings and I nearly jump out of my skin, first thinking it's Sela, then realizing she wouldn't be ringing the doorbell.

I stride to the door, look through the peephole and confirm it's Caroline and Ally, and then unlatch the lock to let them in. I look first down to Ally, giving her as wide a smile as I can muster, bending down to pick her up. Her little arms go around my neck and she hugs me silently. I look over her shoulder, trying for the same smile at Caroline, but her brow immediately furrows with worry.

"What's wrong?" she asks me bluntly, because she can just tell.

I shake my head slightly to her to let her know that I don't want to discuss this in front of Ally. She steps in, brushes past me, and heads into the living room. "Ally . . . come watch some TV for a few minutes. I need to talk to Uncle Beck privately."

I follow her in while Caroline expertly navigates the programming guide until she finds *Dora the Explorer*. I drop Ally down on the couch, ruffle her hair, and whisper, "Be back in a jiff, cutie."

She smiles at me and then her eyes go to the TV and remain glued there.

I walk back to my office with Caroline following. She shuts the door behind her and says, "Where's Sela? Did you two get in a fight?"

I whirl around in surprise. "God, no. We're fine. Perfect. But she's not here and she should be, and I'm worried."

Caroline's look of concern turns to one of amused exasperation. "Geez, Beck. So she's a few minutes late . . . no biggie. Although I think it's adorable the way you worry about her."

"No," I say harshly, and Caroline blinks at me in stunned surprise. "It's not a matter of her being a few minutes late. It's something more than that . . . I can just tell. There's just some stuff that—"

I stop, not even sure what I should to say to Caroline. I'm sure she'd understand, but there's still a tiny part of me that's hoping that Sela will be breezing through the door any minute with a sheepish look of apology on her face.

"Hey," Caroline says softly, stepping toward me with her head tilted. "You're really scared something might be wrong, aren't you?"

I take a deep breath, scrub my hand through my hair, and then let it out in a frustrated sigh. "Yeah . . . there's some shit going on that I really can't—"

"You tell me everything that's going on right this fucking minute, Beckett North," Caroline says with an imperial tone and a look that says she means business. "I'm your sister and I've got your back always. Just like you've had mine, so spill it right now."

My lips curve upward involuntarily, because my sister is fierce and cute all at the same time. She's also been the only one I've been able to turn to in my life who supports me one hundred percent, no questions asked. And I know I can trust her with my worries and the underlying basis for them.

"I don't even know where to begin," I say hesitantly, "because really . . . this story is beyond complex and unbelievable."

"At the beginning," she says calmly as she takes my hand. Giving me a tug, she leads me to the two guest chairs and pushes me down in one before taking the other one and turning it to face me. She sits down, leans forward, and says, "Spill it."

I take a deep breath, hold Caroline's eyes with my own in a steady gaze, and start to tell her the story. "A little over ten years ago, Sela was raped by JT. It's why we invited you over tonight. She was going to tell you, so . . . you know . . . you would have someone you could talk to if you wanted."

"What?" Caroline gasps, jerking backward until she's sitting ramrod straight.

I nod. "He drugged and raped her, along with two other guys. She didn't know it was him at the time, but not long ago identified him by the tattoo on his ribs."

"What tattoo?" she asks curiously.

"A red phoenix. Same one I have . . . I mean had on the back of my shoulder."

"Was it a fraternity thing?" she asks, as she knows the origin of my phoenix.

"Not sure," I tell her truthfully, but then try to steer her back to the full story. Because she's only got the very tip of the iceberg. "But she came after JT looking for revenge. Met me instead, and well . . . you know, things developed. She eventually told me the truth about JT."

"Jesus," she mutters. "What did you do?"

"You don't want to know," I say, dropping my gaze to my lap.

"Uh . . . yes, I do. Are you in trouble? Is she in trouble?"

My eyes drag up to hers, miserable with worry. "Sela plans to go to the police. But first we wanted him out of The Sugar Bowl. Wanted to make the break before he gets arrested so the company could be salvaged."

"And just how did you plan to get him out?" she asks, her voice laced with fear.

"I had him investigated. Found out he owed a lot of money to a bookie and that he doubled down on a UFC fight. I paid one of the fighters to take a dive and now JT owes more money than he has. I offered to bail him out if he signs over the rights to the company."

"Goddamn it, Beck," Caroline yells as she surges out of her seat, then immediately lowers her voice after her eyes dart to the door. "That is some serious fucking criminal shit you just did."

"I know," I say as I sink further into the chair, clasping my hands tight. "But save the lecture right now. I'm worried about Sela because she's supposed to be here and she's not, and she won't answer or return my calls. Something's wrong."

"You think it has to do with JT?" she whispers.

"I don't know," I say angrily, standing up from my chair. "I just know that his deadline to pay the money is looming and he should have given me an answer by now. Couple that with Sela being missing, and I don't know what the fuck to think."

"Okay, calm down," Caroline says as she folds her arms across her chest and starts pacing in front of my desk. "Maybe you should call JT. Just a casual call, ask him if he's made a decision."

"Maybe," I say, because the thought had crossed my mind. I can't even imagine why Sela would be with him, or his having anything to do with her being missing, but still . . . that might help ease my mind.

"Just call him right now," Caroline urges.

"Okay," I say, and pull my phone from my pocket. Just as I pull up JT's contact and start to select it, the doorknob to my office rattles and starts to turn. Caroline and I immediately face the door, prepared for Ally to nose her way in to see what we're doing.

Instead, when the door slowly swings open, Sela's standing there.

Prickles of icy fear sling slide my spine and my heart starts thundering. She's wearing an oversized gray zippered sweatshirt pulled tight around her, one arm held protectively over her stomach. The hood is pulled up over her head and her shoulders are hunched. While much of her face is in shadows, I can see that her eyes are dead and her skin is ghost white.

"Sela?" I say hesitantly, terrified by her sudden presence and odd clothing.

She steps into the office, eyes cutting to Caroline before coming back to me with abject misery clouding her blue irises. She slowly shuts the door behind her, takes a step toward me, and lets out a tiny sob.

"What's happened?" I say as I round the guest chairs and rush to her. Her head drops so I'm only staring at the top of the sweatshirt hood, and I can see her body shaking fiercely. My hands go to the sides of her head and I tilt it upward. With my fingers, I peel the hood backward and gasp when I see Sela's face in its entirety.

Her eyes are bloodshot with tears leaking out and running in rivulets down her face. There's a smear of blood on her jaw and purple marks on her neck.

"What the fuck?" I curse low and my hands pull the sweatshirt apart at the neckline.

Caroline gasps behind me when I open the thick gray material wide.

I stare in utter horror at Sela's white long-sleeved T-shirt that is drenched in blood on the front, most of it dried but with a few patches of shiny wet sticking to her skin. Small spatters spray outward to the shoulders and up her throat, which I can now see is covered in a thick horizontal bruise across the bottom of her throat.

"Fuck, Sela," I say, feeling my eyes start to water. "How badly are you injured? Where did all this blood come from?"

Sela shakes her head vigorously from side to side as she pulls her hand away. Her face tilts up and her eyes meet mine with such sadness I think my knees might buckle.

"Not mine," she says, her voice raspy and filled with pain I'm guessing is from that bruise on her throat.

My eyes cut to Caroline, who stands there with her hand over her mouth, eyes drowning with intense worry. When I look back to Sela, she gives a cough and says, "JT. The blood is JT's."

My stomach bottoms out, and even as horrified as I am by what she's just said to me, I'm filled with so much relief that she's safe that I pull her into my arms, not caring about the blood all over her.

Resting my chin on top of her head as my arms hold her gently, I whisper to no one in particular and expecting no answer in return, "Oh, Sela. What have you done?"

AUTHOR'S NOTE

. . . .

Sela and Beck's dark, riveting love story reaches its epic conclusion in the final chapter of Sawyer Bennett's Sugar Bowl trilogy that began with the novels *Sugar Daddy* and *Sugar Rush*. Look for *Sugar Free,* coming soon.

Read on for an excerpt from

Max

A Cold Fury Hockey Novel
by Sawyer Bennett
Coming soon from Loveswept

. . . .

CHAPTER 1

Max

I stick the nozzle in my gas tank, depress the handle, and flip the catch down to hold it in place. Letting the gas flow on its own, I head across the nearly empty parking lot to the gas station, which is lit up like a bright beacon out here on Possum Track Road. I'm starved and I know my fridge is empty at home, so I'm going to break down and buy some junk food for my dinner. I just won't tell Vale about it, as I don't feel like listening to her bitch at me.

Vale Campbell . . . pretty as hell and nice to look at, but I dread having to hang out with her. That's because she's one of the assistant athletic trainers for the Cold Fury, and most important, working with me on my strength and conditioning. She would most certainly say Snickers, Cheez-Its, and root beer are not on my approved list, and then she'd have me doing burpees, mountain climbers, and box jumps until I puked.

Pulling the door open, I immediately see two guys at the cooler checking out the stock of beer. Both wearing wifebeaters stained with grease and faded ball caps. I, myself, pull my own hat down farther to hide my face, as I don't feel like getting recognized tonight. It's late, I want to get my junk food and get gone. We've got an early morning practice tomorrow.

I turn right down the first aisle, which houses the chips and other such snacks, slightly aware the other two customers are heading to the counter to check out. I keep my back to them just to be safe and peruse the options.

Funyuns.

Potato chips.

Doritos.

Corn nuts.

Reaching for a bag of salt-and-vinegar potato chips, I hear one of the guys drawl in a typical North Carolina redneck accent, "Hey, sweet thang. How 'bout a pack of Marlboro Reds and how 'bout handing me that there box of condoms. The extra large size."

The redneck's companion snickers, and then snorts. I turn slightly to see them both shoot conspiratorial grins at each other, and one guy nudges the other guy to egg him on. While the clerk turns to get the condoms, the redneck leans across the counter and stares blatantly at the woman's ass. The other guy says loud enough that I hear, so I know the woman hears, "Mmmmm . . . that is a fine ass."

Turning my body full so I face the counter, I see the woman's back stiffen and she turns her face to the left to look at a closed doorway beside the rack that holds all of the cigarettes. I'm wondering if perhaps a manager or another employee is in there, and she's hoping for some help.

But she doesn't wait and turns to face the two assholes, squaring her shoulders.

And god damn . . . she's breathtaking. Looking past the red and gold polyester vest she wears with a name tag—clearly a uniform— I see her face is flawless. Creamy skin that glows, high cheekbones, a straight nose that tilts slightly at the end, and full lips that look sexily puffed even though they are flattened in a grimace. Her hair is not blond, but not brown. I'd describe it as caramel with honey streaks and it's pulled back from her face in a ponytail with a low fall of bangs falling from left to right across her forehead.

While she faces the two men resolutely, I can see wariness in her eyes as she sets the cigarettes and condoms on the counter in front of them. "Will that be all?"

Her voice has a southern accent but it's subtle. She looks back and forth between the two men, refusing to lower her gaze.

Redneck number one nods to the twelve-pack of beer he had placed on the counter and says, "That was the last of the Coors. You got any in your storage room?"

"Nope, that's it," she says firmly, and I can tell it's a lie.

"Are ya sure?" he asks, leaning his elbows on the counter and leering at her. "Maybe you could check . . . I could help you if you want, and we could make use of them condoms there."

I'd roll my eyes over the absurdity of that attempt to woo a girl who is way out of his league, but I'm too tense over the prospect that this could be more than just some harmless goofing by some drunk rednecks.

"What do you say, sweet thang?" he says in what he tries to pass as a suave voice but comes off as trailer trash.

"I say there's no more beer back there," she grits out, gives a look over her shoulder to the closed door, and then back to the men.

And that was a worried look.

A very worried look, so I decide that this isn't going any further. Grabbing the closest bag of chips my hand makes contact with, I stalk up the aisle toward the counter as I pull my hat off with my other hand. I tuck it in my back pocket, and when I'm just a few feet from the men, the woman's eyes flick to me, relief evident in her gaze. I smile at her reassuringly and flick my eyes down to her name tag.

Julianne.

Pretty name for a really pretty girl.

The sound of my footsteps finally penetrates and both men straighten to their full heights, which are still a few inches below mine, and turn my way. My eyes go to the first man, then move slowly to the other, leveling them both with an ice-cold glare. With the power of my gaze, I dare both of them to say something else to the beauty behind the counter.

Because I suspect the only sports these guys watch are bass fishing tournaments and NASCAR, I'm not surprised neither one recognizes me as the Carolina Cold Fury's starting goalie. Clearly the lovely Julianne doesn't either, but that's also fine by me.

The sound of Julianne's fingers tapping on the register catches everyone's attention and the two men turn back to her. "That will be $19.86."

One of the guys pulls a wallet from the back pocket of his saggy jeans and pulls out a twenty, handing it to her wordlessly. Now that they know there's an audience, neither one seems intent on continuing the crass game they were playing. At least I think that was a game, but I'm just glad I was here in case their intentions were more nefarious.

Julianne hands the guy his change and they gather their purchases and leave without a word.

As soon as the door closes, her shoulders drop and she lets out a sigh of relief. Giving me a weak smile, she looks at the bag in my hand and says, "Is that all?"

"Uh, no actually," I say as I give her a sheepish grin. "Got distracted by those assholes."

"Yeah," she agrees in a tired voice, brushing her long bangs back before turning away from me to an open cardboard box she has sitting on a stool to her left. She reaches in, pulls out a carton of cigarettes, which she efficiently opens, and starts stocking the rack of cigarettes behind the counter. I'm effectively dismissed and there's no doubt in my mind she doesn't know who I am.

I head back down the chip aisle, grab a bag of Corn Nuts, and continue straight back to the sodas. I grab a Mountain Dew, never once considering the diet option, because that would totally destroy the point of having a junk food night, and then head over to the candy aisle. I grab a Snickers and I'm set.

When I get to the counter, she must hear my approach, as she turns around with the same tired smile. Walking to the register, her eyes drop to the items I drop on the counter, robotically scanning the price of each. I watch her delicate fingers work the keys, taking in her slumped shoulders as she rings in the last item and raises those eyes back to me.

They're golden . . . well, a light brown actually, but so light as to appear like a burnished gold, maybe bronze.

A piercing shriek comes from behind the closed door, so sharp and high pitched that it actually makes my teeth hurt. I also practically jump out of my skin, the noise was so unexpected.

The woman—Julianne according to her name tag—does nothing more than close her eyes, lower her head, and let out a pained sigh. For a brief moment, I want to reach out and squeeze her shoulder in sympathy, but I have no clue what I'm empathizing with because I don't know what that unholy sound was. I open my mouth to ask if she's okay when the closed door beside the cigarette rack flies open and a tiny blur comes flying out.

No more than three feet high, followed by another blur of the same size.

Another piercing shriek from within that room, this time louder because the door is now opened, and for a terrible moment I think someone must have been murdered. I even take a step to the side, intent on rounding the counter.

Julianne moves lightning fast, reaching her hands out and snagging each tiny blur by the collar. When they're brought to a full halt, I see it's two little boys, both with light brown hair and equally light brown eyes. One holds a baby doll in his hands and the other holds what looks to be a truck made of Legos.

Looking at me with apology-filled eyes, she says, "I'm so sorry. This will only take a second."

With firm but gentle hands, she turns the little boys toward the room and pushes them inside, disappearing behind them. Immediately I hear a horrible crash, another shriek, and the woman I know to be named Julianne curses loudly, "Son of a bitch."

One more screech from what I'm thinking might be a psychotic pterodactyl and my feet are moving without thought. I round the edge of the counter, step behind it, and head toward the door. When I step over the threshold, I take in a small room set up to be a combo office/break room. Small desk along one wall covered with papers, another wall with a counter, sink, and minifridge, and a card table with rusty legs and four metal folding chairs.

It also suddenly becomes clear what manner of creature was making that noise that rivaled nails on chalkboard.

A little girl, smaller than the boys, is tied to one of the folding chairs with what looks like masking tape wrapped several times around her and the chair, coming across the middle of her stomach. Her arms and legs are free, and the crash was apparently a stack of toys she had managed to knock off the top of the table.

"Rocco . . . Levy . . . you promised you'd behave," Julianne says in a quavering voice as she kneels beside the little girl and starts pulling at the tape. The little boys stand there, heads hanging low as they watch their mom attempt to unwrap their sister.

I can't help myself. The tone of the woman's voice, the utter fatigue and frustration, and the mere fact that these little hellions taped their sister to a chair has me moving. I drop to my knees beside the woman, my hands going to the tape to pull it off.

Her head snaps my way and she says, "Don't."

My eyes slide from the tape to her, and I'm almost bowled over by the sheen of thick tears glistening but refusing to drop.

"Please . . . do you mind just waiting out there? If any customers come in, just tell them I'll be out in a moment," she pleads with me, a faint note of independence and need to handle this on her own shining through the defeat.

"Sure," I say immediately as I stand up, not willing to add further upset on this poor lady with the beautiful tear-soaked eyes. She clearly has enough on her plate without me adding to it.

Since the release of her debut contemporary romance novel, *Off Sides,* in January 2013, Sawyer Bennett has released more than thirty books and has been featured on both the *USA Today* and *New York Times* bestseller lists on multiple occasions.

A reformed trial lawyer from North Carolina, Sawyer uses real-life experience to create relatable, sexy stories that appeal to a wide array of readers. From new adult to erotic contemporary romance, Sawyer writes something for just about everyone.

Sawyer likes her Bloody Marys strong, her martinis dirty, and her heroes a combination of the two. When not bringing fictional romance to life, Sawyer is a chauffeur, stylist, chef, maid, and personal assistant to a very active toddler, as well as full-time servant to two adorably naughty dogs. She believes in the goodness of others and that a bad day can be cured with a great workout, cake, or a combination of the two.

sawyerbennett.com
Facebook.com/bennettbooks
@bennettbooks